"Don't be naive," he snapped. *"Any man with two eyes would be interested in you."*

"You're not."

Her words, soft and sad, punched him square in the gut. Not interested? Not interested? Oh, but she couldn't be more wrong.

She gasped when he cradled her face. Her lips parted in unintentional anticipation, their surface slick and shining. He ran his thumb across the edge, earning a whisper of a sigh. The noise turned his blood hot. He dragged his gaze from her eyes to her mouth and back, only to find the blue darker. Losing himself in the color, he felt the falling sensation again, leading him to a place warm and safe.

This time there was nothing to stop him. He lowered his mouth to hers, taking the comfort he so badly wanted. For a few moments, he forgot his damaged soul and lost childhood to the taste that was uniquely Delilah.

When the kiss ended, he pressed small kisses to the corners of her mouth. "Still think I'm not interested?" he whispered against her skin.

Dear Reader,

I am so excited to introduce a new trilogy—my first—for the Harlequin Romance line! Delilah, Chloe and Larissa have been best friends since their first day of corporate orientation at CMT Worldwide Advertising. They are surrogate sisters, sharing everything.

Well, almost everything. Delilah hasn't told her friends that she's been in love with her boss, Simon Cartwright, since the day she met him. Thing is, Delilah wishes she weren't in love with the man, since he's so out of her league it isn't funny. He's gorgeous, successful, charismatic. Frankly, the man is perfect.

Or is he? Delilah's about to find out that beneath Simon's suave surface lies a man convinced he's too damaged to find real love. Until now, Simon's been able to bury the horrible hazing incident he suffered in prep school, but a business trip to Boston has finally forced him to deal with what happened. What he doesn't count on is the comfort he takes in Delilah's presence—or the feelings she brings out in him. How can he offer his heart to a woman when he doesn't feel he's man enough to deserve love in return?

Meanwhile, Delilah has grown up believing in a fairy-tale kind of love. If she's going to help Simon heal, she's going to have to seriously reevaluate that definition, as well as how she views the man of her dreams.

Both of them will learn that true, lasting love isn't about perfection. It's about loving the flaws, as well, both in yourself and in others.

Writing this story wasn't easy. Simon's story was a hard one to tell, and I so desperately wanted to do him justice. Both he and Delilah so deserved their happy ending. I like to think I left them in a good place.

I hope you enjoy reading their journey.

Barbara Wallace

The Man Behind the Mask

Barbara Wallace

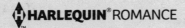

HARLEQUIN® ROMANCE

Recycling programs
for this product may
not exist in your area.

ISBN-13: 978-0-373-74273-8

THE MAN BEHIND THE MASK

First North American Publication 2014

Copyright © 2014 by Barbara Wallace

Printed in U.S.A.

Barbara Wallace is a lifelong romantic and daydreamer, so it's not surprising that at the age of eight she decided to become a writer. However, it wasn't until a coworker handed her a romance novel that she knew where her stories belonged. For years she limited her dreams to nights, weekends and commuter train trips, while working as a communications specialist, PR freelancer and full-time mom. At the urging of her family, she finally chucked the day job and pursued writing full-time—and she couldn't be happier.

Barbara lives in Massachusetts with her husband, their teenage son and two very spoiled, self-centred cats (as if there could be any other kind). Readers can visit her at www.barbarawallace.com and find her on Facebook. She'd love to hear from you.

Recent books by Barbara Wallace

THE COURAGE TO SAY YES
THE BILLIONAIRE'S FAIR LADY
MR. RIGHT, NEXT DOOR!
DARING TO DATE THE BOSS
THE HEART OF A HERO
BEAUTY AND THE BROODING BOSS
THE CINDERELLA BRIDE
MAGIC UNDER THE MISTLETOE

These and other titles by Barbara Wallace are available in ebook format from www.Harlequin.com.

To my fellow Harlequin Romance writers,
a group of women as supportive as they are talented,
and to my two favorite men, Pete and Andrew,
who make life worth living.

CHAPTER ONE

"YOUR BOSS MADE the paper again."

Plop! The folded tabloid landed smack in the middle of Delilah St. Germain's desk, sending papers flying. "Hey! I just organized those."

She threw the two women standing in the doorway of her cubicle a good-natured glare. "Some of us have work to do."

"Some of us would like to point out it's seven-thirty in the morning," Chloe Abrams replied. "We're the only people in the office."

Without waiting for an invitation, she and Larissa Boyd grabbed a pair of chairs from the empty cube across the aisle and sat down. "Besides, we brought coffee."

"Oh-my-God-I-love-you-where?" Spying the two large paper cups in Larissa's hand, she snatched one. "You have no idea how badly I need this."

"No," Larissa said, "but we could guess. How you been, stranger? We haven't seen you all week. You still working on that client pitch?"

"Bartlett Ale? Not at the moment." The potential account had her burning the candle at both ends the past couple of weeks. "But I'm behind on everything else." She lifted off the cup lid and breathed deep. It was still warm, too. "You two are lifesavers."

In more ways than one. Chloe and Larissa had been her best friends since corporate orientation four years ago. Delilah was pretty sure she wouldn't have survived her move to the Big Apple without them.

"Hey, what are friends for if not to keep you caffeinated when you're overworked?" Chloe replied. "What time did you get here anyway?"

"Not that long ago. Six-thirty, seven." Earlier than usual.

Her two friends shook their heads. "There are easier ways to impress the boss than making sure you're in before he is," Chloe told her.

"I'm not trying to impress the boss," Delilah immediately shot back. Not too much anyway. "And you two should talk. I don't see either of you sleeping in."

"Hey, this hour of the day is the only time I can get any wedding planning done, since Tom is always hogging the Wi-Fi," Larissa pointed out. "I came in to surf for bridesmaid dress ideas."

"And I like to beat the line at the coffee shop," Chloe replied.

"So she can have plenty of time to flirt with the barista," Larissa shot back.

"You're just jealous because he gave me a free size upgrade."

"I could so make a joke about that comment right now."

"Please don't," Delilah said. "I already have the image in my head."

Speaking of images.... She reached for the paper Chloe dropped on her desk. Sure enough, there was Simon Cartwright, a third of the way down the column, a beaming blonde draped on his arm.

"Finland Smythe again," Chloe read over her shoulder. "She's lasted a while."

"Two months." Longer than most. Their boss tended to collect girlfriends the way Delilah's grandmother used to collect souvenir spoons. Fashion models, actresses, would-be fashion models and actresses, a literal parade of beauty, every one of them wearing the same thrilled expression.

Who could blame them? Delilah stared at the black-and-white image. What she wouldn't give to be a woman exceptional enough to capture Simon Cartwright's attention.

Like that was possible. Simon was... She nearly sighed out loud. What wasn't he? The man was handsome, intelligent, sophisticated. You could literally feel the energy change in the room as soon as he walked in.

Her laptop had a better chance of attracting his attention.

"Ooh, look, here's an ad for that bridal expo I was telling you guys about." Larissa pointed to a bold-bordered box next to the society column. "You're both still coming with me, right?"

Both Delilah and Chloe groaned. Since getting engaged to her stockbroker boyfriend, Larissa had been in nonstop bridal mode. "Do we have to?" Chloe asked.

"Yes you do. You're my bridesmaids. Besides, it'll be fun. We can look at bridesmaid dresses."

"What happened to the ones you were looking at online this morning?" Chloe asked.

"Not on company time, I hope."

All three women jumped. Delilah quickly turned the paper over. Simon Cartwright leaned against her cubicle opening, arms folded across his broad chest. Like it did every morning, Delilah's pulse skipped a beat at the sight.

Dear Lord, but he took her breath away. It wasn't that he was traditionally handsome. In fact, on a different man, the prominent nose and sensual lips might not work at all. On Simon though…. The strong features fit as perfectly as his custom-tailored suits. Today's number was dove-gray, with a jacket cut narrow to emphasize his long, lean build. A swimmer in college, he still swam laps mornings before work. In fact, the damp curls at the base of his neck said he had just come from the pool.

"Good morning, ladies. I didn't realize there was an intradepartmental meeting this morning. I would have brought pastries."

"Prework coffee klatch," Delilah replied.

"Ahhh. Interesting. The things I miss not arriving earlier. Makes me wonder what other fun activities go on when I'm not here. Speaking of…" He turned to Larissa. "How are the wedding plans going, Ms. Boyd?"

"Very well, thank you," her friend replied.

"Company server isn't bogging down your internet searches?"

"I, um...no?" Her friend's cheeks turned crimson. Ducking her head, she missed the momentary sparkle behind Simon's sapphire eyes. Delilah caught it however; her stomach did another flip.

"Glad to hear it." He turned his attention to Delilah. "When you're done with your coffee klatch, I need you in my office."

Need you. Okay, so he meant regarding business. When said in that rich baritone though, the words still managed to make her insides flutter. Pathetic? Yes. But so was being in love with your boss. If either Chloe or Larissa found out her little secret, she'd never live it down.

Fortunately, she was very good at keeping her feelings hidden. Tucking an imaginary brown strand behind her ear, she gave a quick nod. "Sure thing. Be right there."

"Someone's in a good mood," Chloe noted. "I'm guessing last night went well."

"Maybe." As a rule, she preferred not to dwell on Simon's romantic exploits. Bad enough the gossip columns insisted on rubbing the pictorial evidence in her face. Sitting around speculating only made her feel dumpy and depressed.

She grabbed a nearby legal pad. "Either way, I better get to work. We can gossip at lunch." Although hopefully by then, a new topic would demand their attention.

CMT Worldwide occupied two floors of their Madison Avenue address. The first floor housed accounting and media. Creative and client services, Delilah's division, took up most of the second. As head of the New York branch, and director of accounts, Simon's office sat at the rear of the layout with a sprawling view of the skyline.

Simon stood at the far window bank, facing Madison Avenue. Tall and broad shouldered, with his hands clasped behind his back, he reminded Delilah of a prince surveying his kingdom. Suddenly self-conscious, she smoothed down the front of her blouse. She'd been trying to wear brighter colors these days, in an effort to look more vibrant. Today's choice was a raspberry satin with pleats and cap sleeves that looked far more stylish on the mannequin. Then, everything seemed more stylish when she wasn't standing near Simon. No matter what she wore, she felt impossibly drab and average in his orbit. Still, she smoothed the material anyway, and then brushed the bangs from her eyes for good measure before knocking loudly. Simon hated being approached without notice.

"You wanted to see me?"

He turned around. "Jim Bartlett has narrowed his choice to two agencies. Ours and Mediatopia."

"Fantastic." Doubly so, given how much work had gone into pitching them the past month. Ever since the brewer announced he was looking for a new advertising agency, Simon—and by extension Delilah and everyone else in the agency—had been working like crazy to convince Bartlett Ale that CMT was the perfect choice to sell their beverages. If Jim Bartlett was down to the final two, that meant the agency's hard work had paid off. "When do they make their final decision?"

"End of next week."

Sooner than they originally thought. So why wasn't he smiling the way he normally did when the agency got good news? In fact, the good mood Larissa mentioned appeared to have faded altogether. "Is there a problem?" she asked. "You don't sound very excited."

"Sorry. Bit of a headache. Last night was…" Thankfully, he waved off the rest of the explanation and pulled out his chair. "As for Bartlett, don't start dancing a victory dance quite yet. We have one more hurdle."

"What kind of hurdle?" She sank into the chair across from him. If she had to create another PowerPoint presentation, she was going to scream.

"Apparently, Jim wants to spend some time getting to know each of the candidates on a more personal basis before making his final decision. The agency he likes best wins."

Was that all? "Doesn't sound like much of a hurdle to me." More like a cake walk.

"Careful. We don't want to get overconfident."

"Maybe, but if we're talking a charm contest between you and Roberto Montoya, I'd rather bet on you." She'd seen Simon work a room. The man could sell rat poison to rats if he put his mind to it.

He flashed a row of perfect white teeth. "That's what I like about you, Delilah. You're good for my ego."

Yeah, because he needed a boost from the likes of her. She watched him as he arranged the objects on his desk into neat piles and rows. "So what is it they want you to do?"

"Have dinner with them tonight in Boston

and then tomorrow tour their brewery. We should be back early on Sunday."

"Doesn't sound too difficult. I'll clear your sched— Wait, did you say *we?*"

Simon looked up from straightening his wireless mouse. "Yes, I did."

"You…?" Delilah was pretty sure her mouth did a fishlike movement as she processed his answer. "You want me to go to Boston with you?"

"Yes. Is that a problem?"

"No," she rushed. "Not at all." Overnight in Boston? With him? How could that possibly be a problem? If anything, the opportunity was too good to be true.

"Good, because as my assistant, you'll be dealing with Bartlett as much as—if not more than—I will. Seeing how important this account is, I think it's a good idea for them to get to know you, as well."

"Sure. Yes. Of course. I'll do anything you think will help, you know that." Her excitement was making her babble.

That his lips slowly curled upward in response didn't help matters. "I know you will," he told her. "Makes me glad you're on my side."

Always, she wanted to reply. Fortunately,

she kept her senses and her tongue, settling instead for tucking an imaginary strand of brown behind her ear to cover her blush. "I better go take care of the flight arrangements," she said rising. Then she had to go home and pack. *Oh, dear Lord, pack!* The completely normal task suddenly seemed overwhelming. She was going to have to find Chloe and Larissa to ask them what she should wear. Then, at some point, she needed to tell her insides to settle down. This was a business trip; not a romantic weekend getaway.

"Delilah, wait!" Simon's baritone reached her just as her foot reached the hallway. "Could you also dig up the name of the florist we use? I need to have some roses delivered."

In her mind, Delilah heard a soft *pop!* as her excitement burst. As reminders went, she couldn't do much harsher. "Sure thing," she told him. "I'll get it as soon as I return to my desk."

Just as she had thought; the invitation was too good to be true.

Welcome to Boston, the airport sign read. Enjoy Your Visit.

Good old Boston, Massachusetts. Had it really been fifteen years since he'd visited?

Should have been longer, as far as Simon was concerned. Unfortunately, Jim Bartlett decided to base his operations here, and since he needed Jim Bartlett's business, here he was. Otherwise, he'd never step foot in this godforsaken state again.

His breast pocket buzzed with text messages sent during the flight. Pulling out the phone, he read the top one on the call screen.

GOT YOUR ROSES. GO TO HELL.

At least she got straight to the point, unlike last night, when she insisted on going on and on.

Why did women always want to talk late at night only to get all dramatic because he'd rather sleep than share his feelings? Seriously, what did Finland think he was going to tell her? The truth? He could imagine how well the truth would go over. *Sorry, Fin, but I don't have deeper feelings. I gave them up fifteen years ago.* Here, in Boston. Talk about coming full circle.

At that moment, the town car entered a tunnel, plunging the backseat into shadows. Jarred by the abrupt change, Simon's mind jumped to a different darkness. *Where you going, freshman?*

He shoved the voice from his head. He

didn't have time for this when there was so much riding on his performance.

Damn, but the memories hadn't hit him this hard in years. He hoped it wasn't a sign of things to come.

He ran a hand along the back of his neck, grimacing at the dampness under his fingers.

"Headache bothering you? We could stop for some painkillers."

From her side of the car, Delilah watched him intently. For some reason, the concern in her blue eyes gave him the extra push he needed to regain control. "I've already taken more than I should. Another dose and my liver will stop functioning. Don't worry. I'll be all right. Bartlett won't even know I'm under the weather."

"You better be all right because if I have to carry the conversation, the agency's doomed." She ran a hand around her ear. "I'm not very good at small talk."

"I'm sure you'll be fine. You never seem to have a problem at work."

"Because I'm talking work and it's with people I know. Take away my agenda, and I'm screwed."

Come to think of it, the two of them did seem to limit their conversations to business.

In fact, he couldn't remember the last time they had had a personal conversation. His previous assistants shared everything. Delilah appreciated the value of reticence. Almost too much. He needed to remind her to speak her mind more.

"Well, Bartlett made it very clear on the phone he doesn't want to talk about business at all tonight." Like a male Finland, he wanted to "get to know them as people."

"Yep, I'm screwed."

"I doubt you're that bad. What about when you go out clubbing? You talk to people then, right?"

She gave him a long, odd look. "If you want me to flirt, we're in bigger trouble."

"I don't want you to flirt." He tried to picture his assistant as a femme fatale and failed. "Just be yourself. The key to good small talk is to find some common ground. Shared experiences, that sort of thing."

"What if you don't have 'shared experiences'?"

"Then you put the attention back on them. People love to talk about themselves. And if you get really stuck tonight, you can always ask about beer."

Her response was too soft to hear. "What?"

"I said we're going to be doing a lot of talking about beer then."

"So long as they talk about something." He rubbed the back of his neck again. Damn muscles were as tight as rods. "I don't have to tell you how important signing this account is. With the economy off, clients are scaling back their ad dollars in all three offices. An account Bartlett's size would erase the deficit and keep us from having to lay off employees."

"In other words, the agency's financial future depends on how well you and I socialize over the next two days."

She could have been listening in to a conversation with the board of directors, she managed to quote his father so accurately. "You're catching on."

"Great. So long as there's no pressure."

She didn't know pressure. Yet again, the expectations his father placed on him were almost insurmountable. Thankfully this time he had an ally. So long as she didn't clam up from shyness. If he was going to survive visiting Boston, he needed all the support he could get.

* * *

Other than the insignia flag flying over the front door, the University Club looked like all the other brownstones lining the street—stately and old. Jim Bartlett stood on the sidewalk talking with another man when the cab pulled up. If Delilah were to describe him, she would say he looked like his product. Ruddy-faced, he had a shining bald head and a body shaped like a barrel.

He greeted both of them with enthusiasm, clasping Simon's hand between both of his. "Right on time, even with the baseball traffic. I'm impressed. I just finished betting Josh you were stuck downtown."

"Josh Bartlett," his companion said, sticking out his hand. He was a younger version of his father right down to the barrel shape and matching blue blazer.

"And don't let him fool you. We were the ones stuck in traffic. It's a pleasure meeting you in person, Delilah. My father's mentioned you often."

"In a good way, I hope." She hoped he wouldn't notice the dampness on her palms.

When she told Simon she didn't do small talk well, she wasn't kidding. Too many years of biting her tongue and walking on eggshells made her far better at saying as little as possible. Perhaps if she had a chance to put on the cocktail dress and pumps she packed, she might have more confidence. Unfortunately, thanks to a delay in landing, they were still in her suitcase. She was lucky to have had time to chew a mint and run a comb through her hair in the airport washroom.

Thankfully, the younger Bartlett at least acted like he didn't notice. "Promise, he said nothing but good things. We're glad Simon brought you out to meet us."

"Yes, we are," his father chimed in. "As I explained to Simon last night, I like to know the people I work with, contractors included. A lot of people can give a good sales pitch, but for me to hand over control of tens of millions of dollars, I need to know in my gut that I can trust the person. I want to know they're going to care about Bartlett Brewing Company as much as I do."

"In a lot of ways, Dad still runs the company like a small family business, which means going by intuition."

"And I'll continue running it that way as long as I'm in charge. My intuition made Bartlett Brewing Company what it is today." He looked straight at Delilah. "I don't care how impressive a man's resume is. If he doesn't sit well with me here—" he punched his breastbone "—then he's not the right man for me."

"Then I hope I hit you in the right place," Simon replied.

The brewery owner gave an enigmatic smile. "We'll find out, won't we?" He gestured toward the front steps. "After you, Miss St. Germain."

Delilah wasn't sure what the inside of a private gentlemen's club was supposed to look like, but if she were going to use her imagination, it would look like the University Club, right down to the dark paneled wood and giant lobby chandelier. A grand staircase, lined with presidential portraits—all Ivy League university graduates—led to the main dining room. Delilah tried to be blasé as she ascended, but it was hard. There were a lot of portraits.

"It's on purpose, you know." Simon's breath was warm on the back of her neck, causing goose bumps to ghost across her skin.

"What is?"

"The setting. Bartlett wants us to be intimidated."

"It's working." She felt more underdressed than ever. As if she'd shown up in jeans at a black-tie gala.

Her discomfort got worse as the dinner wore on. In spite of what Simon thought, small talk was not easy. Conversation centered around food and restaurants at favorite vacation spots. Her exotic dining experiences were limited to special dinner dates. Mostly, dining out meant heading to the bar near her apartment. Therefore, she mostly listened and while she did, realized exactly how few special dates she'd actually been on since moving to New York. She wished she could blame the drought on being too busy, but the truth was that none of the men she met were nearly as interesting as the man she worked for.

Simon didn't lie when he assured her his headache wouldn't hold him back. Not only did he match the Bartletts experience for experience, but he also controlled the flow of conversation like a conductor. She watched, impressed as he continually returned the conversation back to the Bartletts and their interests.

"Is this your first trip to Boston, Delilah?"

Jim's question caught her off guard. "Yes, it is."

"Pity you're here such a short time. You won't get to see very much."

"I'm seeing the brewery. What else is there?"

"You have a point there," Jim said with a chuckle.

"How about you, Simon?" Josh asked. "I'm sure you've been the city a number of times."

Simon reached for his wineglass. "Actually, I haven't been back in a long time."

Suddenly something Delilah read in his corporate biography popped into her head. "Didn't you go to school in Boston?"

If she didn't know better, she'd swear her question caused his hand to stutter. "Yes, I did." His voice sounded odd, as well. "Bates North."

"I knew you looked familiar!"

Giving the table a firm slap, Josh sat back in his chair. "Talk about a small world. I think I might have been a few years ahead of you. You rowed, right?"

"Rowing?" Delilah asked. "I thought you were on the swim team?"

"I switched to swimming my sophomore year."

"Oh." From the way Simon's jaw muscle twitched as he raised his glass, she wondered if she'd said something wrong. Surely bringing up school wasn't a mistake though. After all, he was the one who suggested she find common ground to discuss.

Meanwhile Josh turned in her direction. "I played soccer myself. I wasn't exactly the rowing type, if you get my drift." He patted his stomach. "I had a couple friends on the team though. Rowed fours and eights."

"Fours and eights?"

"The number of rowers per boat," he explained.

"I seem to remember some scandal involving the sports teams a few years ago?" Jim said.

"Scandal?" Out of the corner of her eye, Delilah saw Simon reaching for his drink again, his lips drawn in a tight line.

Josh nodded. "Some of the teams went overboard when it came to hazing the freshmen."

"What do you mean overboard?"

"The school didn't share all the details, but I seem to remember something about students being asked to—"

There was a loud clatter as Simon's glass spilled onto his plate.

CHAPTER TWO

"SIMON! WHAT HAPPENED? Are you all right?" The words rushed out of Delilah's mouth in one giant sentence. At the same time Simon pushed away from the table. The glass lay on its side on top of his risotto, what was left of the contents pooling onto his plate.

She reached out to touch his arm only to have him wave her off along with the waitress hurrying toward their table. "No harm done."

"Except to your food," Josh said.

"Serves me right for being such a klutz. Besides, the spill will keep me from overindulging."

"Wish a little spill would keep me from overindulging. I'd just treat it like wine sauce."

"Which is why the two of us are built like beer kegs, and he's not," Jim joked.

All three men chuckled and conversation

shifted to new topics. Delilah did her best to join in, but she couldn't focus. Her brain was too busy replaying what happened. Not so much the spill, but Simon's expression. She wasn't sure if the others noticed, but he'd turned white as a sheet. Like he'd seen a ghost. Even now, while he was acting unruffled by the whole event, his complexion remained ashen. She wanted to ask him if he was ill, but didn't want to make a bigger deal out of the moment now that it had passed.

Still, her concern lingered. After four years of watching Simon interact with clients, she knew the difference between a full-on Cartwright charm offensive and simply going through the motions. Simon might be charming the Bartletts, but she could tell that the special Simon spark had disappeared.

It was his eyes. Normally they reminded her of the prairie sky on a summer's day, bluer than blue. But now the color had dulled, as though a cloud had blown in.

Fortunately, the mishap occurred near the end the meal, and an hour later, the quartet was back on the sidewalk where they began, saying goodbye and making arrangements for the next day's brewery tour. A hearty, two-handed shake accompanied Jim Bartlett's farewell too, she noted, meaning they either didn't notice the subtle change in Simon's demeanor or that it didn't matter. In fact, watching the enthusiastic exchange, she wondered if perhaps she'd let her imagination blow the whole incident out of control. No sooner did the Bartletts head up the sidewalk however, than the smile faded from Simon's face killing her theory. Wordlessly, he opened the door to their town car and waited.

She slid into the backseat, taking pains to move as far to the opposite door as possible. Although he never said anything aloud, based on how he hated being approached unaware, she assumed he preferred a lot of personal space as well, and since he never bothered to correct her behavior…well, she kept up the practice.

A flash of movement caught her eye. Yet again, he was rubbing his neck. After biting her tongue all dinner, she had to ask. "How's your head?"

"Hurts."

That answered that question. "Would you like those aspirin now?"

"What I could use is a drink."

"Really?"

He turned toward her, his expression hidden by shadows. "You sound surprised."

"I am. Last time I checked, alcohol wasn't the best cure for a headache."

"No, but it sure as hell cures other things."

Like what? Whatever it was that spooked him in the restaurant? She wished she had the nerve to ask. Even more so the nerve to erase the gap between them and let him know she was there for him. In the dimness, everything seemed more acute. The sound of his breath exhaling long and slow, the rustle of fabric as he sought to find a comfortable position. Tension radiated from his body. She longed to reach across the seat to rest her hand on his arm to soothe him.

She could only imagine how well that gesture would go over. So instead, she did nothing.

When they reached their harborside hotel, Delilah assumed they would check in and go their separate ways. It surprised her then when Simon grabbed her wrist to stop her from heading to the elevator.

"Aren't you coming?" he asked.

For the second time in less than a day, Delilah imitated a fish. "You want my company?"

"Do you mind? I'm not in the mood for drinking alone tonight."

His smile was almost sheepish, so boyishly winsome, her insides turned soft and warm. How could she say no?

Ten minutes later, she sat in a bamboo fan chair waiting on a glass of white wine. Being close to the water must have inspired the hotel decorator to try a Caribbean theme. With its potted palms and soft calypso music, the verandah bar resembled a tropical hideaway. A New England version anyway. Paper lanterns strung on wires swayed in the ocean breeze. Being a Thursday night, the room was only partially full, mostly small groups of professionals visiting the city on business. She and Simon were the only couple in the crowd.

Only they weren't a couple, she reminded herself. Just employer and employee sitting in a romantic moonlit setting.

She searched around, looking for a distraction. To her left, Boston Harbor stretched black, red and green lights guiding boats to the Atlantic. More lights dotted the horizon, the runway markers for Boston's airport. Delilah watched as a line of planes made their way to their descent. Out of the corner of her eye, she saw the waiter return.

Simon slid her wine across the table toward her, then raised his whiskey in the air. The gesture forced her attention back to him. Not that she needed much force, seeing how she hadn't completely stopped paying attention.

"To getting through dinner," he said.

Delilah frowned at his choice of words. "Wouldn't we be better off toasting to success?"

"That depends on your definition of success."

"You don't think tonight went well?"

"Are you talking about before or after I dumped cabernet all over my tenderloin?" He took a long, healthy drink before speaking again. "I think we can both agree, I've had better performances."

"It wasn't that bad. You recovered nicely," she added, when Simon arched his eyebrow.

"The idea is to not have to recover at all. Not with an account this size."

"Jim Bartlett didn't appear too concerned."

Holding his tumbler by its base, he studied the contents of his half-full glass. "Didn't your mother tell you appearances can be deceiving?"

Her mother had been too consumed by grief

to teach her much of anything. "So, what do we do?"

"Nothing." He set the glass down with a resounding *thunk*. "What's done is done. We start over better and stronger in the morning."

"Well then we really should be drinking to putting tonight behind us," she told him.

"Funny. I thought we were." He raised his glass. "To better tomorrows."

"To better tomorrows," Delilah repeated.

They clinked their glasses and Simon tossed back the rest of his drink. Inspired, Delilah took a healthy sip of her own, hoping the crisp dry liquid would help shake off her concerns.

"Funny how you and Josh Bartlett both went to the same prep school," she remarked, still in the past but at least changing the subject. "What are the odds?"

"Better than you'd think. Sadly, the prep school world is surprisingly small." Either she was imagining things or there was a new edge to his voice. Hard to say since Simon had turned to signal the waitress and she couldn't see his face.

"You said you didn't know him though." Details of their dinner conversation came back. "Jim mentioned some kind of hazing scandal? Do you know what he was talking about?"

"It was nothing."

Okay, there was definitely a change in tone. A newly acquired clip to his words. "Really? Because the way he spoke…"

"I said it was nothing," he snapped. "Stupid kid stuff is all. Certainly not worth the attention everyone's giving the subject."

For *nothing* he certainly reacted strongly enough. "So, the fact you didn't know Josh, is that why… Never mind." The wine, added to the glass and a half she drank at dinner, had loosened her tongue.

"Finish your thought, Delilah."

"Well…" She played with the stem of her glass. "I wondered why you didn't make a bigger deal out of the coincidence, the two of you attending the school, I mean. Didn't you tell me the key to good small talk is to find common ground?"

"I also said to encourage people to talk about themselves."

"Wouldn't this have encouraged conversation? Shared experiences and all that?"

"There are very few experiences from prep school that I wish to remember."

"You didn't enjoy high school?"

"Let's say I prefer to treat high school as though the four years never happened and leave it at that."

His comment surprised her. She'd always assumed Simon ruled whatever kingdom he entered.

Rather than push her luck by asking more, she changed the subject. "I suppose everyone has parts of high school they'd like to forget," she said. "Personally I wouldn't mind blocking out the tenth grade ring dance."

"What happened at the tenth grade ring dance?"

"I caught Bobby McKenzie making out with another girl."

"Doesn't sound so horrible."

"He was my date."

"I stand corrected."

The conversation paused as the waiter returned with their drinks. "You seemed to rebound well enough." Simon continued after the man retreated. "Or are you still carrying a torch for the late great Bobby McKenzie?"

"Oh, I'm definitely over him." Hopefully her cheeks weren't as warm as they felt.

"Glad to hear it."

"Still doesn't mean I don't want to forget the humiliation. When you're fifteen years old, being publicly dumped can be very traumatic."

Simon raised his drink, the glass masking both his tone and his expression. "Trust me, there are far more traumatic things that can happen."

No kidding, thought Delilah. Try losing your father and having your mother turn into a ghost. If only she could forget those years.

"Clearly you were never a fifteen-year-old girl. I was certain Bobby was 'the one.'" That was her mother's fault, too, in a way. "I spent the whole year practicing my married signature. Delilah McKenzie. Mrs. Bobby McKenzie. Over and over, with little hearts over the *i*'s. You'd think I'd have learned my lesson…"

"What lesson?"

"Did I really just say that aloud?" No need wondering if she was blushing this time. Her cheeks were on fire. She pushed her wine to the side. "No more wine for me."

"You still haven't said what lesson you learned."

Not to wear her heart on her sleeve, of course. "If you cover your notebook with stupid doodles, you'll be forced to look at them all year long. I had to stare at those foolish hearts for six more months."

He chuckled in to his drink. "At least you didn't get a tattoo. You could still be staring at them."

"Thank goodness for small favors. Can you imagine? I always wondered what people did when they were stuck with a tattoo they no longer wanted."

"They get it removed."

Delilah shuddered. "Talk about a painful way of forgetting your mistakes."

He turned to look out at the water, leaving her to study his profile. Shadows, cast by the table lantern, flickered on his cheek and highlighted the day's-end stubble that was beginning to show. "Is there any way that isn't painful?"

His eyes glazed over then, and for a second, he disappeared, his thoughts going who knew where. Instinct told her it was some place he shouldn't be. And that he needed a far better distraction than liquor. "Hey." She almost reached out to touch him, only to catch herself at the last second. "How about we go for a walk? My legs could use stretching after sitting all day.

"Or not," she continued when he didn't respond. Her spirits sagged to think she wasn't enough to pull him from his thoughts. "I can go by myself and catch up with you in the morning."

"No," he said just as she got to her feet. "A walk sounds good." Draining the last of his whiskey, he slammed the glass down, then tossed some bills on the table. "Let's go."

The pathway behind their hotel was part of a longer walkway that extended along the entire inner harbor and connected the various docks and piers along the way. On the northeastern end, you had the trade center with its large white cruise ships, while to the northwest you had the naval shipyard, the tops of the USS *Constitution*'s masts visible at just the right angle. In between, ships of all sizes, from beat-up whale-watch vessels to sleek dinner cruisers and private sailboats, moved about all day long.

Delilah hadn't spoken since they'd left the bar, making him wonder if she regretted her invitation. Then again, he wasn't winning prizes for his conversational skills at the moment, either. The whiskey, while warming his insides, hadn't relaxed him the way he'd hoped. There was still an elastic band attached from the back of his skull to the base of his spine.

He couldn't believe Josh Bartlett went to Bates North. Forget what he told Delilah about the prep school community being small; it was still a lousy coincidence. And naturally Jim had to go and mention the hazing scandal....

Thankfully, Delilah didn't make the connection between Jim's comment and his poor reaction. He wasn't sure he could handle her looking at him with more sympathy than she already was.

The hotel pier was quiet at the moment, although a sign posted on a lamppost said the first commuter boat would arrive at 7:30 a.m. There were sailboats floating in slips, their lowered sails tucked in canvas covers, the waves slapping against their fiberglass hulls. The soft sound calling to him, he led her to the end of the main pier where he could stare at the waves lapping the pilings.

Behind him, he could feel Delilah hovering a short distance from his shoulder. Funny, he usually hated people standing close, but Delilah's proximity didn't bother him. In fact, he found knowing she was in his space reassuring, comforting even.

"The water's so black," he heard her say. "Looks bottomless."

So it did. Black and never-ending. He let the gentle noise of the waves wash over him. "There's something very soothing about that idea."

"What? You mean being bottomless?"

"Sure. Knowing you could float underwater forever surrounded by silence."

"You're not planning to jump in, are you?"

He smiled, picturing her concerned expression. "Afraid you'll have to jump in and swim after me?"

"A little."

Her bluntness made him chuckle. Refreshing after so many hours putting up a false front. "Don't worry, I prefer my water a little more chlorinated. I simply meant in general. There's a peacefulness to being surrounded by water."

Good God, listen to him, waxing poetic about swimming. The whiskey must have relaxed him more than he thought. Staring deeper into the depths, he felt the pier sway with the waves, proving his point. He sat down, letting his legs dangle over the edge.

Delilah continued to hover; from the corner of his eye, he could see her leaning against a piling. He patted the concrete next to him. "Come sit down with me."

Leaning back on his elbows, he looked out over the water, listening to the waves' steady cadence as they splashed the objects around them. Once upon a time, he'd latched on to that rhythm to erase the past. Tonight he latched on again, letting it wash the memories back into place.

Over at her seat, Delilah had leaned back on her hands, as well. Not so far back as him, but enough that he could see the length of her thighs and the flash of her pants as she kicked her legs up and down. Her ponytail looked like a long brown tail. As she turned her face skyward, it hung down the center of her back. Made him want to give the thing a tug.

"Do you know, I've been in New York for four years now, and I still haven't gotten tired of seeing the water?" she said to him. "I don't think people on the coasts realize how lucky they are."

"You make it sound like Kansas is a desert."

"No, but watching the Missouri doesn't have the same romantic quality." She turned with a puzzled look. "How did you know I was from Kansas?"

"Your personnel file. I read it when I hired you."

"Oh, I should have realized." She ducked the hair behind her ear, a sure sign she was blushing. Simon was sorry the pier didn't have better lighting so he could see what shade of pink her skin turned.

"Is this the point where I make a joke about leaving home for the Emerald City?"

"Please don't. I heard enough jokes when I first moved here. And before you ask, no, I don't own a little dog or have an Auntie Em."

"Does that also mean I don't have to worry about you clicking your heels three times during a meeting?"

"To go home?" She shook her head, tail swishing across her back. "Definitely not."

"Pretty emphatic-sounding there, Dorothy. Got a problem with Kansas?"

She definitely blushed this time. Even the dim lighting couldn't hide the color. "I'm just really glad to have made it to Manhattan."

"There was doubt?"

"Let's say there was a time when I wasn't sure and leave it at that."

"Okay."

Clearly there was more to the story. Her lowered gaze and pink cheeks said as much, but who was he to judge? Everyone had secrets. Some worse than others.

Smiling, he reached over to pat her hand, silent reassurance that he didn't plan to pry any further. To his surprise, it was he who felt comforted. The warmth of her skin beneath his palm eased his muscles in a way the liquor didn't.

He wondered if Delilah noticed, for she suddenly raised her eyes to meet his. The dim gleam of the dock light reflected in their depths, turning them a richer shade of blue. The color water should be, he thought to himself.

"How come I never noticed how blue your eyes were before?" he asked her.

"I..."

Damn. His comment made her blush again, sending her lashes sweeping downward and blocking his view. He wanted the blue back. There was a serenity to the shade he didn't want to let go of.

"The proper answer is thank you," he said. Shifting his weight, he used his free hand to catch her chin and gently force her gaze upward again. There, that was more like it. "When someone pays you a compliment, you're supposed to say thank you."

"Thank you," she whispered.

"You're welcome." The sea breeze, light as

it was, blew hair into her face, again marring his view. Repeating what he'd seen her do so many times before, he tucked the errant strands behind her ear, his fingers lingering along the outer edge. Those eyes widened, and arousal, that blessed precursor to forgetting, began to curl through him. It surged when he saw her catch her lip between her teeth, as though biting back a sigh....

"Hey! You can't sit there."

Simon jerked back. The voice belonged to a security guard who was strutting toward them. A perfectly timed bucket of water.

"Sorry," the guard said as he drew closer, "but you're going to have to move."

"Right. Of course." He scrambled to his feet, ignoring how the rapid motion caused the pier to shift and throw him off balance. Delilah, who was on her feet, as well, reached out to steady him, but he grabbed hold of a piling instead. "It's time we call it an evening anyway, don't you think?"

From the look on her face, his assistant didn't know what to think. *Can't say I blame you,* he thought as he motioned for her to go ahead of him. Frankly, he wasn't sure himself.

CHAPTER THREE

DELILAH WAS IN the shower trying to clear her head when she heard the phone ring. Grabbing the complimentary bathrobe that hung on a nearby hook, she rushed to answer before the caller hung up. As soon as she saw the Kansas area code on the call screen, her spirits sagged. *Seriously, did you really think Simon would call after the way he bolted from the dock?*

Pushing a smile into her voice, she answered. "Hey, Mom. What's up?"

"Nothing. Thought I'd call and see how you were doing is all. It's been a while."

The last comment earned a guilty stab. "Yeah, sorry I haven't called. Things have been pretty crazy at work."

"Crazy good, I hope."

"Crazy great. Couldn't be better."

The lie rolled off her tongue like butter,

leaving her a little more deflated. She wondered if her mother ever realized that life was always great when she asked. After ten years, the habit was too deeply ingrained to break. They all did it, Delilah as well as her brothers and sisters. They all put on a happy face, lest their mother worry. Because worrying was a negative emotion, and no one wanted to be the person responsible for sending her back into the depression that always seemed to hover nearby.

"In fact," she continued, "I'm in Boston right now." Briefly, she told her mother about Jim Bartlett's request and the last-minute business trip.

"Honey, that's wonderful. Your boss must think pretty highly of you to bring you along."

Her mind flashed back to the dock and the feel of Simon's fingers against her skin. "I don't know what he's thinking," she murmured, her fingers unconsciously tracing his touch's path.

She quickly shook the thought away. "Signing this account means a lot to him. He wants to make sure the Bartletts feel comfortable with everyone involved."

"Which he wouldn't do unless he thought

you'd impress the man. This could be the start of big things for you."

Delilah had to smile. There was no sense arguing the point. Her mother's over-the-top enthusiasm was her way of making up for being mentally missing during Delilah's teen-age years. "You know you're biased, don't you?"

"Just because I'm biased doesn't mean I'm wrong." There was a pause, followed by a soft sniff. "Your dad would be really proud of you. He always said you were his brainy child."

"Thanks." Truthfully, who knew what her father thought; he'd been gone so long her mother's memories had become a mixture of truth and wishful thinking. Still, the reference meant a lot to her mother so she went along. Besides, after tonight's weirdness, the reassurance was nice to hear. "I hope so."

"I know so. Now," her mother said, clearing her throat, "tell me what else is new. How are those two friends of yours?"

Knowing her mother wanted details, Delilah settled back against the mountain of pillows lining the head of her king-size bed and caught her up on everything, including Chloe's barista crush and how Larissa was treading dangerously close to Bridezilla territory.

"I swear she thinks I got myself invited on this trip just to avoid going to another bridal show," she told her mother.

"Some women get a little crazy when it comes to weddings. Which reminds me, don't be surprised if we have one of those around here soon. Danny and his girlfriend are getting pretty serious."

"No way." Delilah almost dropped the phone. Next to Simon, her younger brother was the biggest serial dater she'd ever met. "Did he hit his head or something?"

On the other end of the line, her mother laughed. "Nothing so dramatic. He simply found his missing piece. Isn't that wonderful? I'm so happy for him."

"Yeah," Delilah replied, feeling strangely bereft. "Me, too."

"That's all I want for all of you kids, you know. To find someone as great as your dad."

Better not hold your breath waiting for your middle daughter, Delilah thought.

She spent several more minutes being caught up on the rest of the family and the neighborhood gossip. Finally, after promising to call more often, as well as fielding a plea by her baseball-crazy brothers to send them Boston sports souvenirs, Delilah hung up and tossed the phone beside her on the bed.

As she looked around her hotel room, a sigh worked its way out of her lungs. Any other time she'd be overwhelmed by her surroundings. Things like the super-soft king-size bed and the walk-in shower the size of her entire bathroom back home. Tonight, however, they passed with little notice. Her mother's call left her more out of sorts than ever. She couldn't stop thinking about the fact that Danny, who never committed to anyone for more than a week in his life, was talking marriage, while she was here, alone in a Boston hotel room crushing on her disinterested boss.

This was all her mother's fault. All those years going on about soul mates and missing pieces, making love sound like some grand romantic concept. *"I knew the minute I laid eyes on your dad, he was the missing piece to my puzzle. That one perfect person who made my life complete."*

So complete, she fell apart when he died. Four long years of wishing she'd die, too, while her children struggled to find a way to live without her. *Soul mates*. Delilah hated the word. Hated that she'd been conditioned to believe that kind of true love was possible.

Now her brother had gone and found his soul mate. And what was she doing?

Damned if she knew. The surreal moment on the pier teased her the entire shower. Did she really see heat in Simon's eyes? Or was the whole moment a product of her desperate imagination? If the latter, someone needed to let her body know. Her entire nervous system was awash with awareness.

Tightening the belt on her robe, she got up and walked to the glass. By complete coincidence, her hotel room had the same view as the dock. Through the floor-to-ceiling windows, she could see the lights of departing airplanes. Simon's room was only a few doors down. Was he watching the same view? For that matter, was he even in his room? After the security guard rousted them for sitting on the dock, Delilah had made a beeline for the elevator. The very idea of being in a small space with Simon turned her inside out.

No, the idea of being in a small space following Simon's rejection of you turned you inside out. She saw how quickly he pulled away when the guard arrived. Obviously, *if* there had been a moment, Simon wasn't interested in it continuing. Why would he be? Simon was probably on the phone right now chatting with his socialite girlfriend or some other gorgeous prospective lover. Or having another whiskey to forget the whole evening ever happened.

Her head fell against the glass. Maybe forgetting wasn't such a bad idea after all. Like Simon said, the best thing she could do was start out better and stronger in the morning.

The boathouse was damp and cold. Without sunlight, the air never warmed. Simon's breath made small gray clouds as he dragged the scull from the doorway. Every few feet he had to stop and readjust his grip because his numb fingers wouldn't hang on. At this rate, breakfast would be over, meaning he'd have to sit through algebra on an empty stomach. Crap. This was so not how he wanted to spend his mornings. But, his father insisted he participate in sports. "Sports are an important part of prep school. They teach team spirit as opposed to those damn video games you're always playing." And so here he was, freezing and wet, dragging a stupid boat out of the stupid Charles River.

He didn't see the shadows until they were

on him. One minute he was fine, the next he couldn't move. Someone had his arms pinned behind his back.

A face pushed close, the breath moist and sour from vodka filling his nostrils. "Where you think you're going, Freshman?"

Splash! The cold water surrounded him and Simon felt his lethargic body slowly return to life. It might not be Olympic-size, but the hotel's rooftop pool more than served its purpose. He propelled his way to the other end, his arms slashing the surface. Coach Callahan would have a fit if he saw him now. There wasn't a bit of technique to his strokes. But Simon wasn't interested in technique. It was the burn he craved. He wanted to push himself so hard his brain had no choice but to clear.

Last night's nightmare came out of nowhere. Damn inconvenient, all these memories rising to the surface. Made him stupid, off his game.

He never told anyone about that day in the boathouse. Masking the broken parts of himself the best he could, he took what happened that day and filed them away in a locked part of his brain. Even when the scandal broke years later, he kept the memories quiet and carried on. No one would ever know the truth. How part of him shattered that raw, foggy morning. The world would forever see the Simon Cartwright they wanted to see. And on those rare occasions the memories did intrude and the mask threatened to slip? Well, then he had the pool.

How many times had water saved his sanity?

His fingers brushed the concrete, letting him know he'd reached the opposite wall. Hinging his hips, he pulled his torso down, dragging his memories beneath the surface. When he got low enough, he would flip directions and leave yesterday behind. Once again his life would be organized, the bad memories locked away where they couldn't interfere with the here and now.

A pair of black patent leather flats waited at the pool's edge when he returned, a shiny reminder that not all of yesterday's "issues" could be pulled underwater. He flipped and took another lap, pretending not to notice the shoes or their owner.

Drowning his memories with pleasure was nothing new. He long ago learned the best place for keeping bad thoughts at bay—

outside the pool—was his bed. Fortunately
for him, there was never a shortage of women
willing to join him, although for obvious reasons, he was always careful to keep business
and pleasure separate. Until a second glass of
whiskey blurred the two, that is.

Thank goodness for the security officer.

He waited two more laps before finally
greeting her with a nod. "Morning, Delilah."

She looked different today, though how, he
couldn't say. Outwardly, she looked the same
as ever. Gray slacks, same brown ponytail,
bangs flopping in her face. Had to be the top.
Pale blue silk, it was more fitted and brought
out the blue in her eyes. *Blue like the color
water should be.* Words that should sound
foolish in the morning light, but instead, one
glance told him they remained strangely accu-
rate. Looking up at Delilah's face, last night's
weightless feeling returned. He was falling
and floating all at the same time. Just like
being suspended in the deep ocean.

Oh, for crying out loud, listen to him. He
needed to pull himself together.

"What has you visiting me on the roof at
this hour?" He rested his arms on the pool's
edge and waited while she gathered her
thoughts, hoping her early appearance didn't

signal a resignation. The way he had behaved, he'd be lucky if she didn't slap him with a harassment suit.

She gave him a long, unfathomable look before answering. "Josh Bartlett called."

They were apparently conducting business as usual. Thank goodness. Assistants as smart and capable as Delilah didn't grow on trees. If he had ruined their relationship with last night's insanity, he'd do more than just mentally kick himself.

"Little early for business, isn't it? What did he want?"

She ran a hand around her ear, a habit he remembered finding incredibly fascinating last night. Daytime proved that notion correct, as well. He'd never noticed how long and graceful her fingers were.

"Apparently the Bartlett family has a home on Cape Cod," she told him. "They are throwing a New England clambake tomorrow night and invited us to attend."

"Beer and seafood in a relaxed setting. What better way to catch people with their guard down?" He had to hand it to Jim Bartlett. This need of his to interview agencies on a "personal" level might be peculiar, but the eccentricity had savvy. "You told him we'd love to, right?"

"Not yet."

"Why not?"

"It means staying another two nights, including Saturday night at their beach house," Delilah told him. "I didn't think I should agree until I knew your schedule."

"I have no problem rearranging my life to win this account. You know that."

"I know. I also know how important the account is to you."

"Then why put him off?" Hesitation made them look indecisive, and that was the last image they wanted to project.

"Delilah?" he prompted when she looked away. "Is there a problem?"

"The account team for Mediatopia is also going to be there."

"Why am I not surprised?" He chuckled at Bartlett's audacity. What better way to judge people than to have them mingle with their adversaries? Made his and Delilah's attendance all the more imperative. He was beginning to understand how Bartlett made his fortune, and it wasn't simply because he knew how to brew a good beer. "Tell him I said the more the merrier."

"Are you sure?"

"Why wouldn't I be?"

"It's just that after last night, I wasn't sure you'd be…"

"Up to it?" he finished for her. She nodded. Wow. He must have been more off his game than he thought. "Last night was an anomaly, I promise."

No sooner did he speak than the strangest expression crossed her face, passing too quickly for him to decipher. "Is there something else?"

She suddenly became quite entranced with tracing a splash stain darkening the cement with her foot. "They want us to spend the night."

Of course. "You're worried about spending the time alone with me."

Her face paled. "No, I…"

"It's all right, Delilah." Stupid to think he'd escaped completely unscathed. Letting out a long breath, he hoisted himself out of the pool and made his way to the towel cart. Talking would be good. The two of them could clear the air and move forward.

"Frankly, I don't blame you. I think we can both agree I wasn't myself last night," he said as he toweled off. "The whiskey went to my head and I crossed the line. I'm sorry."

"It's all right. Mistakes happen." Turning abruptly, she headed toward the chain-link fence lining the pool area's perimeter.

"No, it's not all right," he said, following. "I'm your boss, and I have no business making you feel uncomfortable. Ever. I'd hate for an unfortunate mistake on my part to ruin a great working relationship. All I can hope is that you'll accept my apology and let the two of us start fresh."

He wished she would turn around so he could convey to her the full apology in his words. "Do you think that's possible?"

"In other words, you want to pretend last night never happened."

"Only if you're willing to. The ball's in your court." She still hadn't turned around, leaving him to wonder what she was thinking.

After what seemed like hours, she shrugged. "Why not?" she said in an odd voice. "No harm, no foul, right?"

"Thank you." Simon let out a breath as some of the tension bearing down on his shoulders eased. He joined her at the fence, ready to say more when he caught sight of her profile.

Disappointment flashed behind her eyes.

Ridiculous. His conscience was playing tricks on him. Had to be. When it came to his behavior last night, he could see Delilah having many reactions: anger, embarrassment and humiliation, to name a few. But disappointment? Not possible.

"Nothing to thank me for. Last night's completely forgotten." She looked straight at him, wearing the same calm expression she always wore. No disappointment in sight.

"Do you need anything else?" she asked.

Nothing a big fat do-over wouldn't cure. He shook his head. "Not right now."

"Then I'll go call Josh and let him know we can't wait to join them. See you downstairs for the tour."

Simon stayed at the fence watching her walk away. Talk about dodging a bullet. He should be flooded with relief right now. Why then, did he have this overwhelming desire to chase after her before she closed the rooftop door?

Unable to come up with an answer, he headed back to the only place that, while not promising answers, at least offered peace—

the pool. Clearly, he needed a few more laps as everything hadn't been left behind in the water.

"Most of our facilities have switched to brewing our fall varieties, but we're still brewing summer ales here in Boston. For the tourists."

Josh flashed them a grin. "Hope it's not too early for you folks to try some samples."

"Why not? It's five o'clock somewhere, isn't it?" Simon replied.

"Ha." Josh clapped him on the shoulder. "You just named one of this season's flavors."

Delilah watched as Simon stiffened under the younger Bartlett's touch and told herself she didn't care. Simon had made his position very clear this morning. Last night was a mistake. Make that an *unfortunate mistake*. Mustn't forget the adjective, in case she harbored any delusions their interactions meant anything more. Which she couldn't, since Simon had also made it clear that he wanted to start fresh. As far as he was concerned, whatever last night was—drunken mistake, surreal dream, pick a term—it never happened.

Fine. She shot her boss a polite smile when he glanced in her direction. If Simon wanted to file yesterday away, never to be mentioned again, let him. She could pretend nothing was wrong with the best of them. After all, she'd been doing so for the last four years, right? Hell, she'd been doing it since she was a teenager.

Pretending would be a lot easier though if she didn't have to spend the next two days in Simon's company. This morning had been awful enough, being forced to put on an unaffected face while he stood there, his body wet and shining in the sunlight. Racing bathing suits left little to the imagination, and although they spent the entire conversation inches apart, she'd still been able to feel the moisture wicking off his warm body. He'd smelled of chlorine, the chemical scent making it impossible to chase the image away even after turning to the Boston skyline. Dear Lord, but he had looked beautiful.

How on earth was she supposed to spend another forty-eight hours with the man when a simple mental image made her weak in the knees?

Two words. *Unfortunate mistake.*

For goodness' sake, the event shouldn't be that hard to shake. Wasn't like time stood still or she felt sparks when he touched her hand or anything like that. Once you got past the pull of those deep blue eyes, and the heart wrenching disquiet he seemed to wear around him like a shroud, it was just another touch.

Back in the present, Josh was telling the history of Bartlett brewing. At one particular point, he touched Simon's shoulder and she saw her boss stiffen again. If she cared, she'd warn Josh about her boss's need for personal space. Then again, she never truly understood Simon's issue with closeness. Especially since he seemed fine with initiating contact himself.

There was a lot she didn't understand about the man, wasn't there?

"...gallons," Josh finished.

Since he was looking straight at her, she assumed he wanted a comment. "That's a lot of beer," she replied.

Josh grinned. "Actually, we're still in the mash stage so we're still talking grain plus liquid, but either way, we're still talking a sizeable amount of ale."

He beamed with such pride, Delilah had to beam back. "This is the smallest of our brewery locations. It's active mostly for tours and stuff. Hard to believe the original Bartlett used to make his beer in a room at the back of his house."

"Bet the original Mrs. Bartlett was thrilled."

"The first in a long line of tolerant beer widows." Josh grinned again. He did an awful lot of smiling, Delilah noticed, often in her direction. She was beginning to suspect the younger Bartlett found her attractive. After this morning's rejection, the thought was a stroke to her ego, to be sure. If only his smile made her stomach flip-flop the way Simon's did.

"From here, we pump the mash into the brew kettle."

They passed under an archway into another large room with different metal tanks. A bitter aroma clung to the air. "This is where we add the hops."

He motioned for them to step closer to get a better view. As she bent over to read one of the nearby informational plaques, Delilah felt a hand brush the small of her back. The shiver passing down her spine told her the touch didn't belong to her guide. Sure enough, Simon had joined her side.

"The mixture stays here for…whoops, hold on." Josh's cell phone stopped him midsentence. Delilah took advantage of the reprieve to put some distance between her and Simon by pretending to study the other tanks.

"I didn't know you had such a keen interest in beer brewing," Simon said in a low voice.

His breath tickled the back of her neck, the sensation sending goose bumps across her skin. "You're the one who suggested I find common ground, remember? Is that a problem?"

"Not at all. I appreciate the effort."

"It's hardly an effort. Josh is an excellent tour guide."

"Yes, he definitely seems to be working the charm this morning, doesn't he?"

"What was that supposed to mean?" she asked, giving in and looking at him.

"Nothing. Only that he's being very charming."

What did she expect he'd say? *It means I don't want you interested in anyone but me, Delilah?* Nothing was ever going to happen between the two of them. Unfortunate mistake, remember? High time she got over him.

Josh returned, cutting short their conversation. "Sorry to break away," he said. "That was Dad. He's waiting for us in the sample room."

The "sample room" as Josh called it, was a

rustically decorated cafeteria filled with long tables and chairs. There was a long wooden bar along the rear wall, behind which was a line of faux wooden kegs with taps. "Most of our guests consider this room the highlight of the tour," Josh said, ducking behind the bar. "They aren't nearly as interested in making beer as they are in drinking a glass."

"I wonder why?" Simon noted dryly. Before Josh could answer, he stepped up to take the pilsner glasses he was holding out, and handed one to her. "It's Five O'Clock Somewhere?" he guessed with a grin.

"One and the same," Josh replied.

"And if not, we'll pretend," a new voice boomed out.

As though he'd been waiting in the wings, Jim Bartlett entered and immediately joined his son at the tap. Delilah wondered if his absence had been a ploy so his son could feel out Simon on his own.

"On Fridays, we invite the whole company to enjoy a cold one to celebrate the end of another work week," he told them. "Looks like we're starting early today."

Watching the pair pour from the different varieties, she also got the feeling they enjoyed the opportunity to indulge whenever possible.

"They're definitely passionate about their product," she whispered to Simon over her rim.

"Yes, they are. Something we'll need to keep in mind when we nail the account." In a louder voice, he said, "You've got some impressive facilities here."

"I'd never say so outside this room, but Boston will always be my favorite location," Jim added. "It's where the company started. Remembering how small we used to be keeps me humble."

"And proud. It's obvious your dedication to tradition isn't just talk. Delilah and I were just saying how passionate you both are about your product. Hopefully we'll be able to do that passion justice."

"You mean if you get the account."

"Time will tell, won't it?" Simon replied with a confident smile.

"Yes, it will," Jim said, couching his words, as usual. Although his eyes held a little more sparkle than they did last night. Maybe it was the beer, but Delilah didn't think so. The CEO had just gotten a dose of Simon Cartwright confidence, and as she knew only too well, the draw was hard to resist.

The two executives fell into a conversation

regarding the company's other facilities. Delilah was listening when she felt a light tap on her arm. Josh motioned for her to join him near the bar.

"Did you enjoy the tour?" he asked.

"I did. I was telling Simon you're a great guide. I definitely have a new appreciation for what I'm drinking."

"That's the plan." He set his glass down. "I was wondering, since you're staying through to Sunday, it looks like you'll have some time to see Boston. If you'd like, I—"

"Unfortunately, Delilah isn't going to have as much time as she thinks." Simon had returned to his place by her shoulder. "We're going to be stuck working. We have the Javacle account review to prepare for. So, unfortunately, while I'd love to spare her..."

"Work comes first, naturally," Josh replied. "No rest for the wicked."

"Apparently not." Although in this case, Delilah wondered who exactly the wicked one was. "Thank you for the invitation, though. Sounded fun."

As she took a sip of beer, she swore Simon flashed a disapproving frown.

* * *

"Is there a problem?" She waited until they'd left the building before asking.

"I don't know what you're talking about."

"You told Josh we had to work on the Javacle account this afternoon."

"I know."

"Why?"

"What do you mean 'why'? We still have to work whether we're in Boston or New York." Hands in his pocket, he headed down the brewery steps to the sidewalk. "I'm sorry if that disrupts your sightseeing plans. You can always come back another weekend."

Her sightseeing plans weren't the problem. She was more than willing to work. It was his project choice that confused her.

"I mean why did you pick the Javacle account? The review isn't for another month." She knew because she marked the date on his calendar herself. "We don't even have the materials pulled together or the rest of the creative team present." Meaning they couldn't work on the account if they wanted to. "Meanwhile, you just sabotaged an excellent opportunity to score points with the Bartletts."

If she didn't know better, she'd think he had

an ulterior motive. Picking up her pace, she scrambled down the last few stairs to block his path at the bottom. "What gives?"

Simon looked down at her hand. She hadn't realized, but in speaking she had moved her hand so it pressed against his chest. Another attempt to stop his progress. To her surprise, he made no move to break away.

Instead, he squared his shoulders and returned his attention to her face. "Very well. I don't think your spending the day with him is a good idea."

What? "I thought the whole point of this trip was to win favor with the Bartletts. Spending the day with Josh was—is—a great opportunity to do exactly that, isn't it?"

"On the surface, maybe. But looking deeper, you'd be making a mistake."

"I see." Delilah let her hand fall away. As far as she could tell, his argument made zero sense. How on earth would she be making a mistake?

And who was he to decide anyway? Folding her arms across her chest, she decided to ask him exactly that. After all, he had told her to speak her mind. "No offense, Simon, but if Josh is interested…" Which she seriously doubted. "Whether or not I date him isn't your decision."

"Do you?" he asked her. "Want to date him?"

Delilah took a step back. She should want to. From all appearances, Josh Bartlett was a decent guy. Who knows? If she spent time with him, she might develop an attraction. If she was going to get over Simon, she had to start somewhere. "Whether or not I want to date him is not the point. What matters is that I'm the one to decide. This isn't a work matter."

"Ahh, but that's where you're wrong. When your social life crosses with my business, it's very much a work matter. I won't have people saying I pimped out my assistant to get an account."

Pimped her...? "No one is going to say that."

"Really?" At some point they'd resumed walking. Now he stopped to give her a hard look. "You don't think the good people from Mediatopia would be interested in hearing how you spent your Friday afternoon? Especially seeing as how they're flying into Boston themselves?"

"I—" Delilah couldn't think of a counter argument.

"Exactly. Look," he said, rubbing the back of his neck, "the advertising world is a lot smaller than you think. A juicy rumor takes hold and it can dog our agency for years."

Unfortunately, he had a point there. She'd been in the industry long enough to witness how gleefully negative gossip got spread. "In other words, you're protecting your reputation."

"No, I'm protecting yours," he replied.

"How thoughtful of you."

"I'm serious. Who do you think would come out looking better if a rumor got started. The head of the agency or the assistant who didn't say no?"

She weighed his words. She supposed she should appreciate the gesture. Problem was, she was too disappointed to feel grateful. Fool that she was, she had allowed herself to think that maybe he had a more personal reason for not wanting Josh to ask her out.

CHAPTER FOUR

SIMON SUGGESTED THEY cancel the car service and take the water taxi back to the hotel. "After three hours in a brewery, I could use the fresh air," he told her.

Delilah refrained from comment. Interesting though, that his desire for fresh air came right after putting the kibosh on her sightseeing plans with Josh—and that his solution involved a scenic boat trip.

Not that she would complain. Sitting down on a nearby concrete slab, she raised her face to the cool sea breeze. The two of them had walked from the brewery to the Navy Yard where the water shuttle docked. A few yards away the USS *Constitution* stood guard, the pitch on her masts glistening black in the sun.

"So if we aren't working on the Javacle account, what are we working on?" she asked, unable to resist bringing up his excuse.

Simon was frowning at his phone screen. "I'm sure there's some crisis waiting in my inbox. Assuming I can get service, that is. I swear the smaller the ad budgets get, the more demanding the clients become."

"By that logic, shouldn't Jim Bartlett be a piece of cake?"

Chuckling, he sat down across from her. "Bartlett is clearly the exception to the rule."

That he was. "Have you ever had a client like him before?"

"He's not a client yet."

"Still hedging your bets, I see."

"Always." His face twisted into a grimace as he rubbed his neck. It made him look so uncomfortable, her muscles tightened in sympathy.

"Don't tell me you have another headache."

"A little one. I'll live."

Maybe he did need the fresh air after all. She hadn't noticed earlier, but he did look tired. His complexion lacked its usual vigor.

The water taxi arrived and Simon found them a spot by the bow rail where they would have a prime view of the approaching skyline. Unfortunately, all the other passengers had the same idea and crowded the rail. They found themselves wedged between two groups of campers, the crowd pushing them close enough their arms pressed together. Naturally the kids next to her began pushing each other. Delilah immediately turned so she was stood sideways to give Simon extra room. When he turned his own body sideways she saw from the tension in his jaw just how much he disliked being jostled.

"Will there really be layoffs if we don't land the Bartlett account?" Feeling that kind of added pressure would certainly explain why he looked so weary.

"Naturally, nothing's carved in stone," he replied. "Although I know the board asked our California and Chicago offices to put together potential restructuring plans."

"What about our office?"

"Worried about your job?"

"Mine. My friends." With all the strangeness of the past twenty-four hours, she hadn't given the big picture as much thought as she should have.

"Well, you can breathe easy. At the moment, our office appears to be safe."

As well it should be, thought Delilah. Simon brought in more new business than the other offices combined. They couldn't afford staff cuts.

"But," he added, quickly dampening her

relief, "things can change on a dime. The board likes to have their ducks in a row before bringing me into the conversation."

"Really?" Did that mean his father as well? "I would have thought your father would keep you apprised of what's going on."

"You'd think, but my father is very careful to avoid any semblance of nepotism. He doesn't want to treat me any differently than any of his other senior managers."

"Does that mean he'd fire you if you screwed up?" To her surprise, Simon shrugged. "He would?" She'd been joking.

"What can I say, he's old school. CMT is his baby. He doesn't want its reputation tarnished."

"But…" She bit her lip only to get a sternly arched brow in return. He didn't really expect her to finish her sentence, did he? After all, there was speaking her mind and there was biting the hand that feeds you.

"He must be proud of you," she said. A better comment than "you're his baby, too" which was what she had been about to say.

"Says he is. That's half the battle, right?" As though realizing how flippant his answer sounded, he grew serious. "You've met my father, haven't you?"

"A couple times, at the holiday parties." Around the agency, William Cartwright was more legend than real person.

"Then you know he's kind of larger than life."

Like father, like son. "Now that you say it, the picture of him in the lobby does remind me a little of Ernest Hemingway. Like he should be wearing khakis and holding an elephant gun."

"In a different time and place, I bet he would have," Simon said with a smirk.

But what did that have to do with being proud of Simon?

"My father tends to reserve his respect for men like him. Winners, movers, shakers." He boomed the three words. Imitating his father no doubt.

"Well, then he *must* be proud of you," she replied. Simon was all those things and more. "Look at everything you've accomplished."

"Maybe I should send you into his office as my cheerleader. I'm not sure he's nearly as big a fan as you are," he replied with a smile.

Her blush went all the way to her toes. "I didn't mean to gush."

"Don't apologize. Told you, you're good for my ego."

Sure. He wasn't the one who felt like an idiot. The skyline suddenly became ten times more interesting and she turned to the rail. "I doubt your ego needs much fluffing," she murmured.

"You'd be surprised." His softly spoken answer poked a hole in her heart. Surely, he didn't have doubts as to how wonderful he was? She turned her head in time to catch a troubled look flit across his face.

Before she could speak, he shifted positions, and the conversation. "What about you? Midwest girl conquering the Big Apple. What do your parents think of where you've ended up?"

Delilah would rather have kept talking about him than bring up anything about her parents. "My mom says she's happy for me."

"Just says?"

"I think she would have preferred if I stayed closer to home, being a single mother and all. My mom, not me," she quickly corrected.

Simon grinned. "I was afraid you were hiding a secret."

"No secrets," she replied. Only her feelings. "What you see is what you get."

"Nothing wrong with being true to yourself."

"Unless yourself is dull as toast."

"You're not dull," Simon told her. "And even if you were, being dull and true is a lot better than being a fraud."

Only right now she felt very much like one. Everything she really wanted to say she had to bite back. Their proximity made the feelings worse. She swore she could feel Simon's stare peeling back her skin. Discovering the emotions she didn't want seen.

Unable to withstand the scrutiny, she turned to the approaching landscape. "Guess luck is in the eye of the beholder. Anyone who reads the gossip pages would say you're the lucky one—not that I read them very often" She could feel her cheeks growing warm.

Thankfully, Simon either didn't notice her verbal misstep or he didn't care. He turned to rest his forearms on the rail. "What would we do without the gossip columns? It's too bad visibility is so important to keeping CMT relevant."

She was confused. "Are you saying going out is part of some personal marketing strategy?"

"Networking's a lot easier if people already know your name."

"So you go to all these openings and parties so people will recognize you later."

Amazing. She never realized there was so much strategy behind his actions. Now if she could only tell her subconscious not to get excited about the news. Lest she forget he brought dates to all these events. He might attend for business purposes, but she'd bet Finland and her predecessors definitely fell on the pleasure side.

"And here I thought you just liked cocktail parties."

"Nope. Just really good at working a room."

"I know. I've watched you with prospective clients. It's impressive."

"You mean my ability to fake sincerity?" He held up his hand. "It's okay, I'm only half kidding."

"Only half?"

"Well, you do realize two hundred years ago people would call me a snake-oil salesman, don't you?"

She had to laugh at the analogy. "Overstating things a bit, aren't you? I thought snake-oil salesmen sold customers a bill of goods."

"And selling paper towel and soft drinks is different? Sales is sales, sweetheart. Paper towels, snake oil, people. Doesn't matter what you're selling so long as you put on a good act."

Even though he wore a smile, his answer disturbed her. There was an odd tone to his voice. Reproachful, heartrending. Gave her the feeling he was talking about more than simple business. She wished she could see his full expression to see for sure. Sadly though, his face remained locked on the skyline.

The blaring of the boat horn broke her thoughts and Delilah saw the wharf's pyramid-shaped buildings looming close. A soft bump told her they'd docked. "You'll be able to check your email now," she said.

"I will," Simon replied, though he didn't move to take out his phone. Instead the two of them lingered in silence while the passengers around them disembarked. Delilah wondered what he was thinking. She was sad to see the trip end. The past ten minutes had shown her a different side of her boss, a deeper version of the side she glimpsed last night and she wasn't quite ready for it to disappear.

Looking over the railing, she watched as tourists milled around the landing. There were kids running with balloons and ice cream cones, adults looking at walking maps. From the way shorts outnumbered business suits, you'd think it was a weekend. Then again, in summer, Friday afternoon always felt that way. "It's too bad we have to go back to work," she said with a sigh.

"You don't have to."

"I don't?"

Simon still hadn't moved. "There's no reason both of us should be forced to spend a beautiful day stuck inside. You might as well do some sightseeing. Just don't let Josh Bartlett know."

"Well, I do need to find something to wear for tomorrow." It had dawned on her this morning that none of the small amount of clothes she'd packed were suitable for a day on the beach. "Unless you think black pants work for a clambake."

"Only if you want to look like a fish out of water."

"Or clam, as the case may be," she joked. Remembering how out of place she felt at last night's dinner, she definitely didn't want to repeat the feeling a second time. "If you don't mind…"

"Not at all. After all the work you've put into this account proposal the past few weeks, you've earned a few hours. Go. Shop. Enjoy your day."

"Thank you." Excited by her unexpected bonus time, she pushed away from the railing and prepared to disembark. In the middle of shouldering her purse, a question popped into her head. "What exactly is an authentic New England clambake, anyway?"

"Same as any clambake, I suppose, only with fresher seafood. Why?"

"Because I've never been to a clambake before, New England or otherwise, and I want to make sure I dress appropriately." His comments about visibility and marketing made her want to put extra care in how she looked tomorrow night. "What will you be wearing?" She didn't remember him carrying more than a lightly packed bag himself. The Bartletts' invitation must have caught him as unprepared as her.

Simon shrugged. "Not sure. I was going to have the concierge send something up from the hotel boutique."

"Oh." So much for using him as guidance. She started to turn, then stopped again. "I don't suppose… Never mind." It was a silly idea.

"What?"

She waved him off. "It's nothing."

"Delilah, remember what I said about speaking your mind?"

How could she forget? He reminded her every ten minutes.

Simon had straightened, his eyes expectant. Looked like she had no choice. She shouldered her bag yet again. "I was wondering if you wanted to come shopping with me."

What was wrong with him? Yesterday it was flashbacks and nightmares. Today he'd lost his common sense. How else to explain why he was walking around Quincy Market shopping for beachwear with his assistant?

When Delilah asked if he wanted to spend the afternoon with her, he should have said no. After his mistake last night—not to mention today's debacle—the last thing he needed was to risk blurring the line a second time. He had the perfect excuse: work. Yet here he was. What had he been thinking?

Of course, the same could be asked when he made up that idiotic excuse why she shouldn't go sightseeing with Josh Bartlett. Since when did he care about industry gossip? If a rumor did break out, he could squash it before the stories ever reached Delilah.

Much like the way he wanted to squash

Josh Bartlett every time he smiled in Delilah's direction. Who did Bartlett think he was moving in on Simon's assistant?

Then again, since when did he start feeling so damn possessive of his employees? Damn unnerving. Justified though, seeing how he knew exactly how amazing an assistant Delilah could be.

A soft cough interrupted his thoughts. Delilah gave him a small smile. "Don't feel as though you have to spend the entire afternoon with me," she said.

Oh, but he did. He wanted to make up for deep-sixing her plans earlier. Hastening to reassure her, he flashed a smile. "Don't tell me you regret dragging the boss along already." Frankly he was surprised she wanted anything to do with his company after he spoiled her plans. Told him she wasn't that interested in Josh's company after all.

The realization should not please him as much as it did. Nor should he like the blush creeping up her neck.

But it did, and he did, and he didn't want to think about what that meant.

"I only meant that I'm sure there are things you'd rather do than watch me try on clothes the whole time. We could do our own shopping and meet up later."

"Nice try," he replied, shaking his head, "but we both know I'm going to end up hanging around regardless."

"What makes you say that?"

"Because I've shopped with women before."

She laughed. "Something tells me I'm not like your other shopping companions."

No, she definitely wasn't. The other women he knew were obsessively fashion-conscious and self-indulgently extravagant—two traits Delilah definitely lacked.

Another thing—those other women didn't have laughs that slipped over him as easily as hers did. The sound made him feel lighter than he had in years. "Whether you are or you aren't doesn't matter. I'll still have my errands done in about half the time."

"Says you."

She said it softly, almost under her breath, but the challenge came through loud and clear. The craziest thought popped into his head. Went against everything he'd been lecturing himself on the past ten minutes, but what the hell? Why not have a little fun?

"You willing to put your money where your mouth is?"

"What do you mean?"

"I saw on the information kiosk that there's a branch of my favorite men's store on the other side of the marketplace. I bet I can walk down there, find something to wear for tomorrow and be back before you've finished trying on your first outfit."

"Of course you could," she replied. He was about to say something about conceding so easily when she added, "You won't be looking at price tags. Shopping on a budget always takes longer. Try shopping on my salary and see how quickly you shop then."

"Are you suggesting I don't pay you enough?"

"No one at my pay level makes enough."

This time it was his turn to laugh. The woman had a valid point. He was damned if he was going to peruse bargain racks with a multimillion-dollar account on the line. "Fine, we even the playing field. Buy whatever you want without looking at the tag. I'll reimburse you."

"You—you're going to buy me an outfit?" Seeing her flustered expression, Simon almost laughed again. Whenever he caught her off guard, her lips turned into a small O and moved without sound. Made his offer that much more fun to make. "Why not?"

"Shoes and all?"

"Shoes and all. Of course, you realize that now you can't use budget as an excuse." He was curious to see what Delilah would pick once money stopped being an issue. "Do we have a deal?"

Instead of agreeing like he expected, Delilah frowned. "How do you know I won't go crazy and buy a thousand-dollar dress?"

"We're going to a clambake. If you can find thousand-dollar beach clothes, have at it. Although, I know you won't. Your responsible side won't allow it. Now, again, are we on? Winner gets dinner at the restaurant of his choice."

That got her. She immediately folded her arms. "His choice? Someone's awful confident."

"Yes, he is," Simon replied, matching her pose.

"Then prepare to eat your words."

"No I'll be eating dinner, and I have the restaurant all picked out."

In truth, he didn't care who won; he was having way too much fun enjoying the freedom of the moment. As well as this new saucy side of her. She wore it well.

After settling on a time limit, they arranged to meet at Quincy Market's famed Red Auerbach statue. The life-size bronze replica sat smoking a cigar on a nearby bench.

"First person back can take a seat with him and wait," Simon told her.

He leaned closer, for no reason other than he had the sudden desire to move into her personal space. "I'll text you when I arrive."

"No need," she replied, leaning in with a smug smile of her own. "I'll already be waiting."

Their mutual challenges had left them only inches apart. He was close enough he could see the tip of her tongue as it slipped between her teeth. "Why are you doing this?" she asked.

Why indeed? How about because for the first time all day last night's dream was safely filed away. Or because he felt lighter and more relaxed at this moment than he had in years.

"Because" was all he said.

"Not much of a reason."

"Reason enough." He wondered if she knew how erotic it was when she worried her lip like that? Lifting his gaze, he found her studying him, eyes wide with expectant curiosity and yet again, his insides felt that strange end over end sensation.

Startled by the feeling's strength, he stepped back, covering by offering up his most confident smirk. "Better get shopping, Miss St. Germain. It's getting close to dinnertime."

"You do know, I'll be expensing the meal, so even if I lose, you don't really win anything."

"Ah, but you're wrong. I win bragging rights."

Tipping his hand to an invisible hat, he left her to the task.

CHAPTER FIVE

"I CAN'T BELIEVE you selected pizza for your victory dinner." Delilah's ponytail bounced as she shook her head.

It was an hour and a half later and they were making their way to Boston's North End, their respective packages swinging in cadence with their steps. "If you wanted to eat something different, you should have shopped faster," Simon teased. "Not my fault you took so long."

"Five minutes. I took five extra minutes. If there hadn't been someone ahead of me in line at the register, I'd be studying restaurant recommendations right now."

"But sadly, there was someone in line, so you're eating pizza."

He watched as she shifted her packages from one arm to another. She had a few more than he did, thanks to a quick stop at the local sports paraphernalia shop to buy souvenirs and he had to bite his tongue to keep from offering to carry them for her. While offering might be the chivalrous thing to do, it would also lend a datelike feel to the day and, frankly, he'd blurred the line enough as it was.

She nearly dropped a bag. To hell with it, he thought, as he caught the flailing handle. "Let me." Without waiting for an answer, he took some of the heavier bags off her hands.

Delilah's cheeks pinked, but she didn't argue. "Thank you."

"It's the least I can do since you're buying the pizza."

"Technically, you're—" She stopped, leaving him to walk ahead several steps without her. "You didn't pick a cheap restaurant because I said I'd expense the bill, did you?"

"Good Lord, but you're suspicious today," he remarked.

"Sorry, I don't mean to be," she said. "Today's put me off balance. The last thing I expected when I invited you to join me was for you to treat me to a shopping spree."

She held up the bag containing her new clothes. "You didn't have to buy this."

"I know." Same way he didn't have to take the water shuttle or challenge her to a shopping competition. "I wanted to." It felt good indulging someone who didn't ask to be indulged. He smiled thinking of how he'd robbed Josh of enjoying her smile— something he was enjoying far more than he should.

"Consider the dress a reward for a job well done. Like an employee bonus." He would have purchased the souvenirs and dinner, too, but knew she would have adamantly refused.

Delilah considered his words. "A bonus, huh? Too bad I didn't know beforehand. I might have looked harder for the thousand-dollar dress." She smiled, and Simon's insides grew warm. Four years they'd worked together. Why was it he didn't recognize her fantastic smile until today?

"I have to admit," he said, "you surprised me. Your shopping efficiency is impressive. Are you sure you bought an entire outfit?"

"Positive," she replied. "Shoes, too."

So the bags implied. "Then I am doubly impressed."

"In the spirit of honesty, I should have told you that I spent my formative shopping years with three little kids in tow. You should see me in a supermarket. You learn to make fast decisions when your brothers are trying to tip over the display rack."

"I take it you got stuck babysitting a lot."

Her eyes dropped to her shoes. "You could say that."

Years of practice had left Simon able to recognize unspoken words when he heard them and his assistant's clipped answer said a lot. He refrained from asking though. He also knew people held back for a reason. As badly as he wanted Delilah to continue, he wouldn't push.

After several silent steps, Delilah spoke again. "My mother had a hard time after my father died. She needed a lot of help."

"I didn't realize," Simon replied. "When you said single mother, I assumed…"

"He was killed in a car crash coming home from work."

"I'm sorry. How old were you?"

"Fifteen. And since I was the oldest…"

She picked up the slack in responsibility. Again, unspoken words said a lot, making Simon wonder how much slack she carried. Fifteen was far too young to become an adult. "I'm sorry," he repeated, thinking they were two of the most inadequate words in the English language.

"Stuff happens, right?"

Simon recognized the tone; it was nonchalance in the face of hardship.

"What else can you do?" she asked.

The answer was nothing. You did what had to be done. You pushed aside your pain and your lost childhood, and you stayed strong.

Interesting how both their lives changed irrevocably at age fifteen. Maybe that's why he felt such a bond with her from the start. On some unconscious level, they understood what it was like to see your innocence snuffed out in one flashing instance.

It was an unfair parity. After all, Delilah didn't shoulder any blame. Misfortune had thrust upon her. She never had a chance to speak up, to stop reality from crashing down around her.

Unlike him.

"Things are better now, I take it?" An obvious question, seeing how she had moved to New York.

"She— That is, things got better while I was in college."

She did it again, tried to cover and minimize the situation, but Simon caught the slip anyway. "Do you visit them much?" he asked.

"Not as often as I should. Don't get me wrong—I love my family."

"But you need your space."

A shadow crossed her features. "Exactly," she said in a softer voice. "I'm sure I sound like a bad person for saying this, but I can be myself out here. There's no pressure."

"Pressure?"

"To be the Delilah my mom wants. You know how parents are."

Did he ever.

"Listen to me," she continued. "You ask about my father, and I get all melodramatic. I'm sorry about that."

"Don't be. You weren't that melodramatic."

They fell back into silence, the only sound the soft *smash* of Delilah's shopping bags hitting her legs. "For what it's worth, you're not a bad person," he said eventually.

"Now who's being good for whose ego?"

"I mean it." Reaching over, he grabbed her wrist, forcing her to stop and face him. "Seriously. From what I see, I don't think you could ever be a bad person."

What you saw was what you got. There weren't many people in the world you could say that about, himself included. Simon's appreciation for her grew.

"So…." To his disappointment, she slipped her wrist from his fingers. The sudden loss left his hand so empty, he almost reached for her again. "Where's this restaurant you're taking me to?" she asked. "We've been walking forever."

"Won't be long now. We're in throwing distance in fact."

"Assuming the restaurant is still standing," she remarked. "Fifteen years is a long time."

Except in some instances, when fifteen years wasn't long enough. He shook the darkness off. This trip was about good memories. "It's still here." He wasn't completely flying blind; he'd checked the web for the listing. Surprised him how many landmarks still existed. Evidence that the more things change, the more some stayed the same.

One more corner, and Simon's pulse picked up in nostalgic excitement. Mangia's looked just as he remembered. There were a few changes, of course. The awning was newer, and the owners had added outside seating, but the green-and-red neon sign still hung over the door bright and garish and condensation fogged the front windows just like in his memories. He wondered if the insides still smelled like fresh bread and wood smoke. He didn't have many good prep school memories, but pizza at Mangia's was one of the best.

Stepping inside, Simon took in the brightly painted walls with disappointment. He missed the bunches of dried herbs; they'd been discarded in favor of a modern interior that was, in his opinion too cream-colored and plain.

The row of booths in back hadn't changed though. In the middle one sat two teenagers, boys not more than thirteen or fourteen, a half-eaten pizza between them. He smiled at the familiar picture.

"My roommate freshman year had a cousin who told us about this place," he said to Delilah. "We'd take the T here on Sundays, get a large Mangia special and spend hours debating whether the truth was really out there."

"Excuse me?"

"Science fiction conspiracy."

"You were a sci-fi geek?" She sounded shocked, like he'd told her he was an alien himself. Proof he had become so adept at playing his role that not even a glimmer of the boy he was remained. Today, however, he wanted that boy to return. For some unexplained reason, he needed Delilah to see him. To know the him that had existed once upon a time. "Sci-fi geek, computer game aficionado." So many weekends enthusiastically arguing imaginary facts. "We had a great time that year."

"Only one year? What happened?"

A loaded question if ever there was one. "I got older, and had to put childhood behind me." He hoped that would be answer enough.

Delilah nodded. "Happens," she replied. Her face, normally so open and bright, grew sober. Thinking, no doubt, how her own life changed at that age.

The hostess led them to a table by the window. With its wine bottle candleholder and red-and-white tablecloth, it couldn't help but feel romantic, despite the casual surroundings. As she took her seat, Delilah tried to picture a teenage Simon gorging on pizza and debating cult TV. Quite the change from that version to the adult sitting across from her. She wondered what precipitated the transformation. Something significant, since he had gone from fun-filled Sunday afternoons to never wanting to think about prep school again.

Funny how freshman year of high school was such a benchmark for both of them. Never in a million years did she expect to share common ground with Simon.

But then, neither did she expect to be sitting in an off-the-path Italian restaurant or spend the afternoon retail-racing her boss. Last night's surreal atmosphere seemed positively natural in comparison.

She had to admit, she liked this version of Simon Cartwright. Liked him a lot. She would miss him when Monday rolled around and things returned to normal.

"You're frowning," Simon said. "Is something wrong?"

"I was just thinking how today didn't turn out the way I expected."

"Really?" he asked as he held her chair. "How so?"

The comfort level for one thing. One would think that after last night, everything between them would feel awkward and tense, but no. The more time she spent in his company, the more relaxed she became, to the point where she almost forgot Simon was her boss. Especially those moments when he stood close and time seemed to pause. Then she forgot everything.

She'd pay for those moments come tomorrow when reality returned.

"There's no one thing," she replied. "The day was different is all. Good different."

"You're not still disappointed I disrupted your plans with Josh?"

"I liked the company I had just fine." She waited for a blush to join her blatant honesty, but none came. Only a smile, which Simon returned.

There was another of the day's surprises—her cheekiness. She found herself saying things she would never dream of saying when they were in New York.

Since Simon selected the restaurant, Delilah willingly handed over the reins when the waiter arrived for their order. To her amusement, he ordered enough pizza for the entire agency. "How much do you expect me to eat?" she asked him.

"I'm simply making the most of my victory," he replied. With a grin, he explained the circumstances to their server.

"A bet, huh? I'll bet you won't be making that mistake again," the man teased.

"I've learned my lesson. Although—" she leaned in after the waiter walked away "—as bets go, this is the most lopsided one I've ever known."

"That a complaint? I can always take back my offer."

"Don't you dare. I deserve that dress. I'll

have you know I worked my behind off on this account pitch."

"Yes, you did. But then you always do. We're—I'm lucky to have you."

Delilah didn't care if the word change was simply a case of semantics; when he switched *we* to *I,* her heart gave a little jump. "Thank you."

"I'm also sorry," he continued, "if these last-minute plans ruined your weekend."

"They didn't."

The waiter returned to set a plastic pitcher of cola on the table. Delilah noticed that Simon avoided alcohol when ordering. To ensure last night didn't repeat itself, no doubt. Again, he waited until the man left before filling their glasses.

"No exciting plans?" he asked.

"Afraid not. Well, I am supposed to attend a bridal expo with Larissa Boyd tomorrow. But I'll survive."

"I can tell. You sound so disappointed about missing it."

"Caught that, did you?" she said with a laugh.

He handed her a glass. "What do you have against bridal expos?"

"Nothing. They're fantastic if you're planning a wedding. If you're not, however, they can be somewhat…"

"Boring?"

"Repetitive. She's already dragged me to two of them, and I'm sure I'll get dragged to more. How about you? Did Bartlett's plans ruin your weekend?" He was, after all, the one with the busy social calendar.

"Nothing pressing. A fund-raiser at the Met."

Thinking of what he had said, about social events being more work than social, she wondered if he was as relieved as she was to get out of the commitment. Although in his case, the change in plans meant missing more than the fund-raiser. "I hope Finland isn't disappointed."

If he found her comment coy—or nosy—she couldn't tell from the shake of his head. "Doubt it. She and I aren't on speaking terms at the moment."

"You're not?" Her heart gave another little leap. "But I thought… Didn't you send flowers yesterday?"

"A failed peace offering."

"Oh." So they were only fighting. Much as it pained her, she tried to sound sympathetic for his sake. "Maybe once she's had some time to cool off, you can try again."

"I don't think so. The fight would have happened sooner or later anyway. We had different definitions of our relationship."

"How so?"

"She thought we had one."

Pretty big difference. Their order arrived saving her from making a comment. Two large pizzas bubbling with cheese and spices. Delilah's stomach growled. She hadn't realized how hungry she was until she smelled the mozzarella. "Dear Lord, that smells heavenly," she said, inhaling. Simon slipped a piece onto her plate, and she attacked it with gusto.

"Now, that's what I like to see," he said. "A woman who's not shy about eating."

Popping a dangling piece of cheese in her mouth, she told him, "Smells too good to be obsessive."

"It's still refreshing. Most of the women I know refuse to be seen eating in public. Did you know Finland refused to order anything in a restaurant other than mixed greens and sparkling water?"

"Sounds like you need to date a different type of woman."

Great. Now he would think she meant someone like her. Which she did, but she didn't want him to know that.

Focused on folding his pizza slice in half, Simon missed the implication. "Wish I could," he replied. "Except a different kind of woman would have even bigger expectations than Finland."

"About what? Relationships?"

"Relationships, life. Funny thing about women who aren't superficial. They tend to go for men who aren't superficial either."

"You're not superficial," Delilah replied. It hurt to hear him make such a harsh comment about himself.

"Don't be so sure. I've certainly heard the accusation often enough."

"I wouldn't call your ex-girlfriends the most reliable of judges."

"Maybe, maybe not." He paused to take a bite. "But have you stopped to think you aren't, either?"

It was almost as if he wanted her to think he was a shallow phony. Problem was, his argument went two ways. He was just as prone to bias as anyone else. If he wanted to keep her at arm's length, then so be it, but she refused to believe he was as empty as he claimed.

"And sometimes people have more substance than they think."

"Even the Tin Man had a heart," she teased, throwing his Oz reference back at him.

"Terrific. I'll get a big red watch to hang on my chest to prove my substance. Maybe I can get a medal to prove I'm not a coward, too."

Ouch. They were still talking in jest, right? Because he sounded so bitter it stung.

"Knock it off, Kevin."

The nasal-pitched whine killed any opportunity to ask. While they were eating, three more teenagers had joined the pair in the booth. By this point, their pizza and cola were gone, except for a pair of uneaten crusts. One of the newcomers, an older boy twice the size of the original occupants, began breaking off pieces and tossing them in one of the younger boy's face. "You're not supposed to waste your food," he said.

Delilah looked to Simon. He'd noticed too and sat watching with tight-lipped annoyance.

"I'd kill my baby brothers if they did something like that," she said. "You weren't like that when you came here, were you?"

"No." His jaw clenched with displeasure.

"Good." Hopefully the boys would leave soon, so she and Simon could go back to their conversation. She wanted to know why he sounded so bitter.

"Kevin, I said to quit it."

"Quit it, quit it. You sound like a parrot. Hey, Polly, wanna cracker? You wanna cracker, Polly?"

"Hey!"

The entire restaurant stilled when Simon's voice rang out. Delilah watched as he rose to his full height. Shoulders squared, he leveled the boys with an ice-blue stare. "He asked you to stop," he said in a low voice. "So stop." There was no doubt he expected his order to be obeyed.

Across the room five mouths dropped wide-open. They matched her own. Never, not once in four years, had she heard Simon's voice grow that cold. No matter how grievous the error.

Finally, Kevin stood up. "Let's get out of here, guys. This place is lame anyway."

They left in a pack, with sounds of "What's his problem?" being muttered under their breath. She noticed Simon kept his eye on one in particular, the young boy who'd been the target. He lagged a few feet behind the others, and while his friends shot glares in Simon's direction, he kept his eyes on the ground.

"Sorry about that," Simon said once the door shut. He sat back down. "I didn't mean to be so abrupt."

"Are you kidding? I'm glad you spoke up," she told him. "If you ask me, those bullies deserved more than that."

"Too bad it won't make a difference. Ten to one they'll start up on the kid before the end of the block, in retaliation for ruining their fun. And he—" Simon tossed his napkin on the table with apparent disgust. Delilah wasn't certain, but it looked like his hand was shaking, as well. "He'll let them like a pathetic coward."

"Little harsh, don't you think?" And completely out of proportion with what happened. "He's just a kid."

"Doesn't matter. He should have fought back. Be a man, instead of letting himself take it and be humiliated. There's no coming back once that happens."

Now his reaction truly was out of proportion. Just like that, the day's easy atmosphere disappeared, replaced by a tension Delilah couldn't explain. Simon had gone back to rubbing his neck, his grip tighter than ever as he massaged the muscles. In the back of her mind pieces were trying to click together.

She'd seen him react oddly twice now. With these boys and last night in the restaurant. When the Bartletts mentioned hazing. Three times if you count the way he shut down her questions in the bar.

And every time his eyes had the same hard, haunted look to them.

"Did something happen in prep school?" The question was out before she could think twice.

Simon stilled. His features darkened. Delilah rushed on before she lost her nerve. "I only ask because you seem…"

"Prep school was fifteen years ago." Like last night, he shut down the discussion.

His tight-lipped response answered her question. Something *had* happened. Hoping to draw him out, she reached across the table only to have him move his arm move out of range. "It's getting late," he clipped. "Do you mind if we skip dessert?"

"Sure," Delilah replied. "Anything you want."

What she really wished she'd skipped was opening her big fat mouth.

In the end, whether she'd asked her question or not didn't matter; Simon's reaction stuck in her head the whole taxicab home. She couldn't stop thinking of how dark his face got when she mentioned prep school. Didn't take a rocket scientist to know she'd hit a nerve. That *all* the events this weekend had hit nerves. What's more, Simon all but confirmed her suspicions by retreating into tense silence. Question was, what had happened to upset him so much?

Back in her hotel room, it didn't take her long to find the information on the internet. She need only type in the words *Bates North* and *Hazing* to find several articles. "Hazing Scandal Rocks Prestigious Prep School" read the headline. The articles reported how several of the school's varsity sports teams were accused of hazing underclassmen as part of a team initiation. Members of the rowing, football and track teams were disciplined. The article didn't say much more; victims didn't grant interviews.

Delilah read the date. The complaints were lodged two years ago. Long after Simon had graduated. Still, that didn't mean a tradition didn't exist. Someone had to have started it. And the article did mention the rowing team…

You were a member of the rowing team, right?

I switched to swimming my sophomore year.

I put childhood behind me.

He should have fought back.

There's no coming back once that happens.

An unsettling, ugly scenario formed in her mind. She thought of the boy in the restaurant, shuffling behind, the assurance harassed out of him, then thought of a fifteen-year-old Simon. There was only one question left she hadn't answered.

Which side of the problem had he been on?

You don't just walk onto the varsity squad. You've got to prove you're one of us. You gotta show us how much you love the team. And there's only one way I know how to prove that...

In his darkened room, Simon stared at the lights of Logan Airport and let the whiskey burn the back of his throat. The hotel pool was locked so liquor and a hot shower were his only choices.

This is what he got for tripping down memory lane. Once the door cracked open, everything pushed through, both good and bad.

God knows, the bad had been pushing to get out since last night.

So what does he do? Spend the day with his assistant. He had no business relaxing. Relaxing only led to letting your guard down and then...

Arrgh! He jammed his fingers through his hair. Why the hell couldn't he keep his thoughts under control? For crying out loud, he'd kept the damage hidden until now.

Poor Delilah. Stuck watching him slip up yet again. All because he was a selfish ass. Again. His control in that area had apparently slipped too. His guard was down on all fronts. After all, he hadn't been attracted to Delilah before this weekend.

Now, he laughed sadly, his attraction warred with his memories for his focus. Whenever he thought of those warm blue eyes, his body got hard as a rock.

The more he thought about it, maybe seeing those teenagers had been a good thing. They reminded him he had no business nursing an attraction to someone as decent and real as his assistant. No business at all.

He poured another drink, and drained the contents in one sip. Thirty-six more hours. All he had to do was get through Bartlett's party, then he could go back to New York where, hopefully, things would go back to normal.

So long as he didn't do something stupid.

CHAPTER SIX

THIS WAS ALL Chloe's and Larissa's fault. If their voices hadn't been in her head telling her to jazz up her wardrobe, she never would have bought something so out of character. She would have gotten capri pants or Bermuda shorts, something more fitting her personality. But no, she had to go with this. In the store, the cream-and-yellow sundress seemed fun and sophisticated. Today it simply looked short. Her thighs looked like two giant white columns. She tugged at the skirt trying to make it longer, but no luck. What had she been thinking?

About Simon, of course. What else was new? His challenge put her in a frivolous mood. That, however, was before. Before their conversation at the restaurant. Before he wigged out over a bunch of teenagers. Now, like the sundress, frivolous no longer fit.

There wasn't a doubt in her mind that something happened while Simon was in prep school. Hazing, bullying, *something*. Whatever the name, the event had affected him deeply.

Astonishing. He was the last person she would guess could be shaken deeply by anything. The Simon she knew was always so collected and in charge. But if this trip proved anything, it was that there were facets of Simon's personality she didn't know existed.

Including a dark side.

A knock sounded on the door. Delilah's stomach dropped. Shoot! Her rambling thoughts cost her the chance to change. Taking one last look in the mirror, she tugged on her skirt again and hoped she didn't look too foolish.

The first thing she noticed was that Simon did far better in the shopping department. Somehow he managed to find a linen shirt the exact same blue as his eyes. It was a struggle to not stare at the smooth expanse of skin exposed by his open collar.

The second thing she noticed was that his mood hadn't improved. When they said their good-nights, he'd been tense and he was still tense now. It didn't matter how casually he propped himself against the door frame; Delilah could see the rigidity in his muscles.

That and the fact he wore a pair of dark sunglasses.

"Good morning," she greeted. "Sleep well?"

Instead of answering, he looked her up and down. The scrutiny left goose bumps on her skin.

"This is what you bought yesterday?" His voice had a new husky layer, rough spread over smooth. Combined with dark sunglasses, it gave him a weary air.

"Yes, it is," she replied, so wanting to own her decision with confidence. If only his stare weren't driving her crazy. "You don't think it's too—"

"You look fine." Hardly a confidence builder. "Are you ready to go?"

"Almost. I just need to slip on my shoes." Another iffy decision as the wedges emphasized how white and exposed her legs were.

"Fine. Don't be too long. I'll meet you at the checkout desk." Pushing himself upright, he headed toward the elevator.

Well, that wasn't awkward at all. Apparently instead of starting fresh, like yesterday, he was simply going to shut down.

She missed yesterday's Simon already.

The car ride was worse. Not only did they spend the first several minutes of the drive in awkward silence, the luxury sedan Simon rented felt like a clown car. The bucket seats were positioned far too close together and Delilah could swear she felt the hairs on his forearm brush against her bare leg every time they shifted. In some weird personality shift, he didn't seem all that affected by the proximity. Meanwhile she longed to put as much distance as possible between their bodies. She was practically pressed up against the door and it still wasn't enough. On top of everything, her skirt had ridden up, and she was afraid to readjust it, in case the movement called attention to her legs.

"How's your head?" she finally asked.

"Do you realize you've asked me that same question the past two mornings in a row?" Simon replied, eyes staying on the road.

"Because you've had a headache since we arrived," Delilah pointed out. Apparently remnants of yesterday's cheeky Delilah remained. "Not to mention the fact you showed up wearing sunglasses."

"Of course I'm wearing sunglasses. We're heading to the beach."

"In the hotel corridor. I thought maybe you were experiencing some kind of light sensitivity."

That got him. He let out a defeated sigh. "I didn't sleep well last night."

"Was it because of what happened in the restaurant?" She had to ask. Goodness knows the altercation had her up half the night speculating. From the way Simon's hands tightened on the steering wheel, it appeared her guess was correct.

"If you don't mind, can we not talk about last night?"

"I looked up the news articles on the hazing scandal. The articles said the rowing team was involved."

The knuckles grew whiter as his grip tightened. "That was long after I graduated."

"Was it?" Then why was he strangling the life out of the car? "I'm sorry. I don't mean to be nosy…"

"Then don't."

"I can't help it." She paused, before adding, "I'm worried about you, Simon."

He sighed and some of the fight faded from his demeanor. "I'm sorry. I don't mean to be a jerk. It's just that there's so much riding on today. I have to make sure I give a good performance which means I can't afford any distractions."

For the first time since the drive began, he looked in her direction and smiled. "Not even well-meaning ones."

"I understand." He was right. This wasn't the right time to press. "And I'm sorry, too." And not only about pushing the issue.

"Thank you." Simon's relief was palpable. "By the way, I apologize for being so abrupt earlier. You look very nice in that dress. I should have said so."

"Well, you are now." And the simple way he spoke made the words sound ten times as sincere. Pleasure ran through her. "Thank you."

Hoping to hide how much the comment affected her, she turned toward the window. The Bartletts couldn't have asked for a better day for their party. The sky was clear but for a few cotton-ball-size clouds puffing their way toward the horizon.

"I still don't truly understand what Bartlett thinks he's going to gain inviting both agencies to the same party," she said. "He's not going to pit us against each other in beach volleyball or something crazy like that, is he?"

"Wouldn't put it past the man," Simon replied, offering his second smile of the morning. "Honestly though, I've been thinking about what his plans might be. Ultimately, I think he wants to get us relaxed enough that we'll show our true colors and reveal whether or not we'll be easy to work with."

"Getting us to relax I understand. But why both agencies together?"

"Easier than throwing two parties?" he replied with a smirk. "Seriously, he probably feels having both agencies there at the same time makes comparing easier for people. Wouldn't surprise me if he's got guests at this party whose job is to chat up each agency and report back."

"So much for relaxing," Delilah muttered.

"You're going to do fine. Pretend the party's one big networking event."

"Networking, huh? Have you forgotten about me and small talk?"

"Again, you'll do fine. The lady doth protest too much."

"I beg your pardon."

"Small talk," he said as he merged into a new lane. "You certainly managed to keep Josh Bartlett interested."

"Oh dear Lord, I forgot about Josh. I lied to him about having to work all day yesterday."

"You didn't lie. You had a change of plans. Josh is a big boy. I'm sure he'll understand."

"I hope so," she replied.

"Of course, if you're afraid you'll trip up, you might consider keeping your distance."

Delilah absorbed what he said. "So let me get this straight," she said finally. "I'm supposed to relax and be myself, but not too relaxed because I have no idea who's a regular guest and who's been sent to spy on us."

"Right."

"And to be on the safe side, I should also make sure I don't talk to one of the few people I'm actually comfortable talking with. That about cover it?"

"Sounds good to me."

"Ugh!" Delilah's head fell back against her headrest. "Why don't you just take me back home now?"

"Believe me. If I could, I'd turn this car around and take us both back right now."

What Jim Bartlett called a beach house was really a compound of small buildings dominated by one huge, gray shingled house on a hill.

"Looks like the beer industry is thriving," Simon noted dryly.

As the view unfolded in front of her, Delilah fought to keep her jaw from dropping. "What happened to Yankee austerity and tradition?" Delilah replied.

"It made half a billion dollars, that's what happened."

They pulled into a circular drive which was already filled with cars. Evidently Jim Bartlett spied them arriving because he stood on top of the front step. "Welcome to Bartlett Bay!" he boomed in welcome. "I hope you brought your appetite."

"Absolutely," Simon replied.

Delilah's jaw almost dropped again watching her boss emerge from the car with a smile to match his host's. Amazing. It was as though someone flipped a switch, transforming him into the Simon she watched every day. It really was a very skilled performance. Her heart couldn't help sinking a little at the realization.

"In fact," she heard him say, "we made a point of skipping breakfast."

"Good thinking, because if there's one thing we like more than beer around here, it's food. I'm pretty certain we bought out the pound."

"Pound?" she asked, confused.

"The lobster pound," Jim explained. "Where we buy our seafood. By the way, you look lovely this morning, Delilah."

"Thank you."

The older man gestured to a housekeeper who Delilah just realized had been standing nearby. "Put their bags in the second guest house, will you, Sandra? Josh mentioned you were a swimmer so we put you in the closest cottage to the pool," he said to Simon. "He's off giving your fellow New Yorkers a ride in the boat, but he should be back shortly."

"Nice of him to make their trip worthwhile," Simon remarked. "Be a shame for them to drive all the way up here for nothing."

Jim laughed. "Well played, Cartwright. You might be a cocky son-of-a-gun, but you're growing on me. Now if you'll excuse me, I better go check on how the bonfire's coming along. Party's round back. Follow me."

"You're growing on him," Delilah repeated once their host was out of sight. "There's a good sign."

"We hope. Could mean he didn't like me much before."

"Now who couldn't like you after the entrance you made?"

She meant the comment as a tease, a compliment to his ability to charm despite feeling under the weather, but Simon didn't smile. His face was the picture of seriousness. "Yeah, who couldn't."

"Hey!" In a reverse of last night, she reached for his wrist as he was about to walk away. "I know you don't feel like yourself today." And that it was adding to his stress. Couldn't be easy knowing people's jobs depended on your ability to work a room. "If it's any consolation, I think you're going to knock 'em dead."

Something unreadable crossed Simon's features. Knowing his dislike for uninitiated touch, she assumed he would pull away. To her surprise, he reached out and brushed the hair from her cheek, his fingers lingering on the curve of her jaw. His skin was still cool from the car's air-conditioning. The sensation turned her insides warm. "I don't deserve you," he said in a tired-sounding voice.

Delilah forced the moment to stay light, even though her insides were fluttering. "No, you don't, but you've got me anyway."

For a moment, he looked as though he might say—or do—more. Delilah's mood sank when his hand dropped away. "Time to go party," he said.

The performance, it appeared, was back on.

* * *

Jim had already disappeared from view so they followed the sounds of laughter and music along a gravel path to the back of the house. *Larissa would die,* Delilah thought stepping onto the verandah. The place looked like the photos in her friend's wedding magazines. The pool alone was a showpiece with its blue-and-copper pattern tiles and potted palms. Beyond the backyard, tall sea grass waved in the breeze. And beyond that, Delilah saw a thin strip of beige beach framing the Atlantic Ocean.

"Wow," she said out loud.

"What did I tell you? Beer pays."

She studied the clumps of guests. They were a mixture of young and old, all comfortably but expensively dressed. "Wonder which one will be the first to grill us?" she asked, making sure to keep her voice soft.

"I think your answer is coming through the grass."

"Simon! Delilah!" Josh Bartlett waved and jogged over.

Delilah never would have recognized him. He wore a damp golf shirt and flip-flops. Beads of sweat dotted his forehead. With a grin firmly in place, he lifted off his baseball cap to wipe them away. "We were wondering when you'd get here."

"You know Cape traffic," Simon said.

The two men shook hands. "That I do. It's lucky you got here at all. You know Roberto and Carl from Mediatopia, don't you?" He pointed to the two men who'd joined him. They both wore similar linen shirt and khakis combinations to Simon's although neither man's shirt draped their bodies quite the same way.

The taller of the two spoke first. "Of course we do. Good to see you again, Simon."

"Roberto. How was your drive?"

"Same as yours. Slow, with lots of traffic."

"I just took them out in the boat to see the bridge. If you'd like, I can take you out for a ride later."

He addressed the invite to Delilah. "Sounds great," she said. "Right now though, I wouldn't mind getting a cold drink."

"Me, too. Come on, I'll show you where everything is."

Hand finding the small of her back, he steered her toward the bar area on the far side of the swimming pool. Remembering Simon's warning, Delilah looked over her shoulder to check his reaction. Unfortunately, he was busy talking with Roberto.

"What's your poison?" Josh asked her. "Pale ale, dark ale?"

"Iced tea. I don't like to drink in the heat," she explained when he frowned. "Gives me a headache." Mentioning the word headache made her think of Simon and she looked in his direction again.

"Relax, I'm sure he won't mind if you enjoy yourself. After all, this is a party."

"Only you and I know it's not your average party."

"You mean the whole interview game my father's playing. I wouldn't worry too much." He handed her a glass before reaching into a nearby ice bucket for a bottle of his own. "Your boss is the one under scrutiny, not you."

"Well, in that case, I doubt they'll find much to scrutinize."

"He's definitely slick. In and out of the office."

I wouldn't be so sure. "You've been reading the gossip pages."

"Once or twice," he replied with a shrug. "Guy's got quite a social life. Must make working for him a challenge. What with his being on the town all the time."

For an offhanded remark, it came out pretty darn forced.

All of a sudden, it hit her. *Unbelievable.* In a flash, all her nervousness disappeared. Doing her best not to laugh, she quickly raised her glass. Not quickly enough however; Josh caught her smile.

"What's so funny?" he asked.

"If you want an employee's perspective, you just have to ask."

"Oh." His cheeks, already flushed from the heat, grew redder. "You figured me out."

"You weren't very subtle."

"No, I pretty much suck at subterfuge. I'm sorry, it was my father's idea."

"No need to apologize. Although, I do have to ask one question." She looked up from her drink. "Did you offer to take Carl sightseeing, too?"

"Baseball. And for the record, he wasn't nearly as pleasant—or as attractive—company."

"I'm flattered."

"You're welcome." He started to take a drink only to pause. Realization broke over his features. "You didn't really work yesterday, did you?"

Busted. She scrambled to come up with an

excuse. Oh, what the heck? They were both being honest. "No," she told him. "I didn't."

"In other words, we're both a couple of liars."

"Bad ones at that," Delilah added.

The two of them broke into laughter. Over on the other side of the pool, Simon had parted ways with the Mediatopia reps and was making his way around the pool. She watched as he got halfway only to be approached by a different guest. Realizing she should probably explain the whole story before he arrived to join them, she caught her breath.

"In all fairness, when Simon made up that excuse, he was thinking of me," she told Josh. "He was concerned people would think I used my 'feminine wiles' to get the account."

"Simon said that?"

"I told you, he was trying to protect my reputation. Keep in mind, he and I both thought you were asking me on a real date."

Josh pursed his lips. "You don't say. And Simon said he was worried about your reputation."

"No need to sound so skeptical," she replied. "You wanted to know what Simon's like as boss, right? Well, there's your answer. He's a boss who cares about his employees."

"And whose employees clearly care back."

It was a statement, not a question, and not a very subtle one at that. Feeling cornered, the contents of her iced tea suddenly became very interesting. "He's a good boss."

"That's not what I meant."

"No, but it's what *I* meant," she shot back. Defensiveness bristled along her spine. She didn't care what kind of interview game the Bartletts were playing; her feelings for Simon were off-limits. "I know what you're implying and there's nothing going on."

"If you say so."

"There isn't," she insisted. It took effort, but she managed to keep the disappointment out of her voice while she emphasized the point. "He is my boss, nothing more."

Josh appeared to acquiesce. "My mistake."

"I won't hold it against you," Delilah replied. "You're only doing your job."

"More like botching. Thankfully, I'm much better at pumping beer than people," he said with a grin.

"I don't think I'd be much better," she assured him. In fact, she knew she wouldn't. When he first pulled her aside, she thought she might be able to ask him about the hazing scandal at Bates North only to realize doing so would call attention to Simon and lead to more questions. Her curiosity would have to wait until she got home.

Josh polished off his beer with a loud *ahh* before reaching back into the ice bucket for a bottle of water. "Since I've blown my cover, guess that means I can sit back and relax. Watch you spend your day fielding questions."

"Gee," Delilah replied. "Thanks."

"No problem. If you want, I'll even help you get the ball rolling." He offered an elbow. "Come on, I'll introduce you to some of the other interrogators...."

"I have to admit, this is the first time I've had to spend a day eating lobster on the client's dime to win an account," Roberto said, his smile brilliantly white. "I could get used to the idea."

"You and me both," Simon replied. He was only half listening, the other half of his brain watching Delilah and Josh giggling over cocktails. He did not like the way Bartlett looked at Delilah earlier. It was way too similar to how Simon had been looking at her.

How on earth did he ever think the woman

was mousy with that body? The dress she bought fit like a damn glove, a breezy, flowing glove that shifted with every bump and sway of her hips. When she answered the door this morning, it was all he could to not grab hold of those curves and make them sway some more, preferably while pressed up against him.

So much for his putting his attraction away. Meanwhile, Delilah just put on her "I'm blushing" face. What was Bartlett saying to her?

"How many of these guests do you suppose are ringers?" he heard Roberto ask.

"I'd say one hundred percent of them."

"My guess, as well. Appears we're in for an eventful visit. Good luck to you."

One eye still on Delilah, Simon offered similar wishes. He spent a few more minutes being cordial, then excused himself, saying he wanted to get a drink. All of a sudden he'd gotten very thirsty.

"By the way," Roberto said as he started to walk away, "from one friend to another, watch out for the woman sitting under the green umbrella. Old broad's got a thing for younger men."

"Thanks for the tip," Simon replied. Which Roberto no doubt hoped would lead to Simon flirting shamelessly. He made a mental note to find out about the woman before speaking with her.

Such a beginner's mistake; so unlike his competitor. Simon was distracted, but he wasn't an idiot.

Now Delilah was blushing again. She and Josh were getting way too chummy. Hadn't she listened to a word he'd said yesterday? Someone needed to interrupt before things got out of hand.

Halfway around the swimming pool, his progress ended when a large athletic-looking man grabbed his arm. "Simon, right? You went to Bates North?"

Stupid idiot, he thought, staring at the hand on his arm. He could feel his muscles beginning to tense and prepared to jerk away. It never crossed his mind there would be guests who'd attended Bates. Of course there would be. In a rarified circle such as this, at least ninety percent graduated from one of the boarding schools.

The man introduced himself, a vaguely familiar-sounding name. Whoever he was,

he'd obviously been told about Simon because
he immediately launched into a trip down
memory lane involving more vaguely familiar
names and the latest fund-raising campaign.

"...in the end I decided to give the full
amount. I know after the hazing scandal a
lot of alums pulled their support, but really,
what's the big deal, right? Not like they
weren't pulling the same sort of stuff when
they were there. I mean, look at Chip Amato.
He was infamous for the stuff he used to do
on the crew team...."

Simon's insides froze. It was a name he
hadn't heard in fifteen years. One he never
wanted to hear again.

*You've got to show us how much you love
the team...*

He managed to fake a smile in spite of the
bile in his mouth. "Yeah, Chip did some crazy
stuff." Horrible, crazy stuff.

Clearly what's-his-name thought it all a big
joke. "Tell me about it. I heard about this one
kid he cornered in the locker room... Hey, are
you all right?"

No, he was pretty sure he was going to
lose what little he had in his stomach. "The

heat," he lied, coughing. "I need to grab some water."

"I'll let you head to the bar then. We can count on you for a donation though?"

"Sure," he managed to spit out. "Send the stuff to my office."

He returned to his mission, hoping he didn't look too shaky as he broke away. The line about water wasn't a lie; an empty stomach, the sun and Chip Amato's memory decided to pound their way into his brain. What he really needed was Delilah. He needed her steady presence. The warm, safe feeling he got when looking in her eyes. Then he'd feel better.

Only one problem. When he got to the bar area, Delilah had moved on.

Without Delilah to center him, he was forced to make the rounds on his own. Sixty minutes of small talk with half a dozen people, all thinking they were being subtle about pumping him for information. He even spoke with Roberto's supposed cougar, who it turned out, was actually mourning the death of her partner—her *female* partner.

While making a note to repay the Mediatopia exec the favor, he scanned the beach for a cream-and-yellow sundress. Where the devil had she gone? He'd specifically told her not to spend too much time with Josh and what had she done? Take off with the man. The barrel-chested millionaire was probably grinning his cheeks off at her right now. Dammit, Delilah wasn't supposed to be fielding grins; she was supposed to be here. With him.

He headed toward the bonfire. Jim Bartlett headed in the same direction. If he couldn't find Josh and Delilah, he could distract himself by making small talk with the senior Bartlett.

Halfway along the beach path, Delilah's laugh floated up from the dock, hitting him square in the gut. Looking to the dock, he saw Josh helping her out of his speedboat.

As soon as Delilah spied him, she waved. "Simon! Guess what?" she exclaimed when she spotted him approaching. She looked amazing. Windblown cheeks, hair damp and wild around her face. Her sandals dangled from her fingertips, leaving her padding in dainty bare feet. And again with that dress swaying back and forth. Simon's body hummed with arousal.

"We saw a shark!" Her smile lit up her face

adding to the sexiness. "His fin anyway. He couldn't have been ten feet from the boat."

"Sand shark," Josh replied. "Must have followed the Gulf Stream up here."

At the sound of Josh's voice, Simon's arousal turned to annoyance. The guy had helped Delilah out of the boat already. There was no need for his hand to hover near her back.

"Sounds like I missed a fascinating trip," he said, making sure he flashed a wide smile. "Would you mind if I steal my assistant back for a minute? I need to chat with her."

"Don't keep her too long." A handsome, silver-haired man jumped out of the boat and joined them. He slipped his arm around Delilah's shoulders. "They'll be serving the lobsters soon."

"Thomas and his wife, Louisa, are going to teach me the proper way to crack the claws."

"All in the wrist," Thomas joked.

"Something tells me I'll still end up with lobster juice on my bib." Delilah's smile faded. "What's wrong?" she asked.

Wrong? How about the fact that he needed her and she was off gallivanting with someone else? Tired of watching people touch her, Simon had replaced Thomas's arm with his and was steering her toward the beach. "Looks like you got over your small-talk phobia pretty quickly," he said when he was certain they were out of earshot.

"What? Oh, you mean Thomas and Louisa? Aren't they sweet? They remind me of my grandparents."

"And Josh? Does he remind you of your grandparents, too?"

"Don't be ridiculous. By the way, we completely misjudged his invitation the other day."

Simon dropped his arm. "Is that so?" Sure didn't look it to him.

"Turns out the only reason he asked me out was so he could grill me about you and the agency. He gave Carl, Roberto Montoya's assistant, the same treatment."

Same treatment, his foot. He bet Carl didn't come back looking all wind-teased and sexy. "And you believed him?"

"Why shouldn't I? What would be the point in lying? Besides, you should have seen him trying to be subtle. Completely transparent."

"I bet."

Delilah's face drew into a frown. "What is that supposed to mean?"

"Nothing." He didn't feel like rehashing the

argument, even if anyone with two eyes could see the man was interested in more than information.

"Obviously it's something or you wouldn't feel the need to drag me onto the beach. I know you said not to spend too much time with Josh…"

"Oh, so you do listen to me."

"Of course I listen to you."

"Well then, if you can tear yourself away from sightseeing, I'd appreciate it if you focused on the reason we're here."

"I am focused. Thomas and Louisa happen to be Jim Bartlett's oldest and closest friends. If anyone's vote of confidence in this matters, it's theirs."

"I see." Simon stopped to study the bubbles in the surf. "How did you meet these great contacts?"

"Josh introduced us."

Of course he did.

Simon rubbed at the knot in his neck. He sounded like a petulant child, but he couldn't help himself. Hearing her laugh like that with Josh sent yesterday's possessiveness into overdrive. She was supposed to be by *his* side, dammit.

She was by his side now. They'd walked as far as the private beach would allow. Standing at the water's edge, he watched as the surf kissed Delilah's bare feet, the bubbles splashing up and over the pale pink skin. She pulled her foot back, her toe drawing a line in the sand that was quickly erased by the receding wave. If only everything could be erased so easily. Like childish conversations.

Like the past.

"I thought getting to know them better would help our cause," Delilah said in a soft voice.

He hated that she thought she needed to apologize. "Forget I said anything," he told her.

"No problem." Her toe drew another line. "I'll add it to the list."

"List?"

"Of things I'm supposed to forget this weekend."

That list. Damn thing must be a mile long by now. Delilah's attention remained trained on the surf. Simon's hands itched to catch her jaw and turn her face to his. He suddenly needed to see her eyes. The dark Atlantic was a poor substitute.

"He's interested in you," he heard himself say.

The comment won him what he wanted; she looked up, her blue eyes wide. "Don't be ridiculous. I told you, he asked Carl out, too."

She was the one being ridiculous. Josh might have entertained Carl, but he definitely didn't smile at him like he was a piece of cake too good to eat. "Trust me. I know interested when I see it. Josh Bartlett is interested."

"Oh."

That's all she had to say? *Oh?* A sour taste rose in his mouth. "Are you interested in him?"

"Would it matter?"

He should have said no, but staring into her blue eyes, he could only think about how he'd found the calm he'd been looking for. The falling sensation gripped him, leading him to a place warm and safe.

Before he realized what he was doing, his fingers brushed the hair from her face. Her skin was damp from the sea spray. The salty scent rose up like an erotic perfume. "You're my assistant," he told her.

"What does that mean?"

"It means…" Squeezing his fingers into a fist, he turned away. "It means nothing."

His head needed distance to think. A few feet away, the beach and sea grass met on a small flat. He headed there and sat down. A warm presence by his shoulder told him Delilah had followed. "What's going on?" she asked. "You're not acting like yourself."

Simon almost laughed at the inadvertent irony in her statement. "This weekend's getting to me is all," he answered. It was, quite possibly, the understatement of the century. "This whole game Bartlett's playing… It's too much. I'm tired."

"You are?"

Of course she would sound surprised. She saw the same Simon Cartwright as the rest of the world—the man who breezed through life. The winner, the charming champion. Fifteen years later, the promise he made to himself in the boathouse held strong. No one knew the flawed reality.

Taking off his sunglasses, he pressed the heels of his hands to his eyes, trying to keep the thoughts from escaping. God, but things were so much easier when he was in New York.

"What was easier?"

He didn't realize he'd spoken aloud. Intending to answer "nothing," he turned around, only for the response to die on his tongue when he saw the concern on Delilah's face. Real, honest concern that came from caring.

It suddenly dawned on him that Delilah might be the closest thing he had to a real friend in this world. No one else would put up with his behavior this weekend. The way he jerked her around from hot to cold and back. She deserved more than a vague answer.

"Playing Simon Cartwright," he said.

Her expression clouded. "I don't understand."

"It's an act, Delilah. The charm, the confidence, all of it."

"What are you talking about? You might be a little off your game…."

"It's all a game," he corrected. Her need to defend him, even though futile, left a warm spot in the center of his chest. "I'm nothing more than a really good actor. A snake-oil salesman giving the people what they want."

"I don't believe you," Delilah said. "I've known you for four years."

A voice laughed in his head. Shame, bitter

and sharp, rose in his throat. It choked him till his vision blurred. "No one *knows* me, Delilah," he said, breaking away. "Not the real me. They haven't for fifteen years."

"I'd like to."

She'd been asking for an answer since this morning. Did he dare give her the one she wanted? He couldn't bare the idea of letting her down. On the other hand, her knowing would definitely sever whatever it was going on between them this weekend.

How he'd love to have someone understand.

"Simon?" Her hand rested on his arm. The touch eased some of the tightness in his throat. "Who are you?"

This was it. Once the words were out there would be no turning back. He turned so he wouldn't see the disappointment flooding her eyes. "A coward." The word made him sick to say. "A weak, pathetic coward."

"No." Her whisper was hoarse. She was fighting him, but there was no escaping the truth.

"I'm sorry, Delilah." She had no idea how sorry. He went to move, but she tightened her grip on his arm.

"No," she repeated. "You can't say something like that and walk away. Why on earth would you think such a thing? What happened?"

Simon fought the urge to run as the memories of that day flashed before his eyes. "You don't want to know."

"Please…"

"Hey, you two! Lobster's up! Better get up here before there's nothing but shells."

For once, he was relieved to hear Josh's booming voice. Surrendering Delilah's touch, he slipped on his sunglasses. The time for comfort had ended. It was time to play Simon Cartwright again.

Delilah watched Simon trudge his way back to the party. Even though she had used the word *performance,* she didn't realize how much of a performance it was until she watched him slowly pull himself together. With each step, his spine unfurled, as though he were calling on some inner strength to take control until, by the time he reached the top of the pathway, the Simon Cartwright she knew so well appeared once more.

Pathetic coward. She'd heard those words before. Last night at the restaurant. She thought them the first time he said them, and she thought them more so today. How on earth could she believe such a thing?

Yet, the hollow tone of his confession said he believed every word.

He said he'd been hiding himself for fifteen years. Meaning they were back to prep school again, and the ugly scenario she conjured up last night. Although this time she had a feeling she knew which side of the altercation Simon had been on.

Poor, poor Simon, she thought watching his form disappear from view. *What did they do to you?*

CHAPTER SEVEN

JIM BARTLETT MEANT it when he said they took their food seriously. Delilah couldn't remember the last time she saw so much food outside an all-you-can-eat buffet. There was lobster, steamed clams, barbecued chicken and every salad imaginable, all piled high on tables beneath flickering tiki lamps.

"Those little legs have some of the sweetest meat in them," Thomas told her. "Key is to not be shy and just suck the meat out."

She stared at the eight bent legs protruding from her cracked lobster and patted her stomach. "I don't think I can manage another bite," she told him, pushing her plate aside. "No one told me 'clambake' was New England code for 'stuff yourself silly.'"

"We take dessert seriously, too," Josh said, coming around her shoulder. "Hope you saved room!"

Delilah managed a smile. A table away, Simon shot her a knowing look as the younger Bartlett sat down next to her.

"I have to agree with Delilah," he said. "The food was amazing."

"The whole trip is," Roberto chimed in. "You've been incredibly gracious hosts."

"Have no fear," Jim Bartlett said. "Whoever wins the account will have more than enough work to make up for my generosity."

"Duly noted," Simon replied.

Another time, Delilah might have been impressed by how at ease Simon appeared, but their conversation on the beach had changed everything. Now she found herself analyzing his every move. With his eyes still hidden behind his sunglasses, there was no trace of the pain she saw earlier. He laughed and joked as though these people were old friends, appearing so at ease in his own skin. Surely, a person couldn't fake such confidence, could they?

Then again, hadn't she done her own share of faking all those years she'd lied about her mother? And hadn't she followed Simon's lead tonight, as well? As her laughing with Thomas and Louisa proved, it was very easy to bury what you didn't want to deal with.

Suddenly she needed a break. Excusing herself, she headed to the guest cottage so she could splash cold water on her face. It didn't help. The splash of the water reminded her of the surface of the water, and when she closed her eyes she saw Simon's tortured expression. The image tore her insides to shreds.

She returned to the pool area just in time to find Josh heading toward the cottage. "Hey," he greeted. "Dad took your boss and Roberto for a walk on the beach. I think it's the final date before the elimination round."

"Thanks for letting me know."

"No problem. For what it's worth, the corporate romance appears to going well. Simon's and my father's, that is. I won't be surprised if Roberto loses out." He leaned against the back of a nearby chair. "Is everything all right? You haven't seemed yourself since we got back from the boat ride."

Okay, so maybe she wasn't as adept as Simon at masking her inner turmoil after all. "May I ask you a question?"

"Sure," he replied. "Although if it's about the agency selection, I can only give my impression. Unfortunately, I'm not in on the final decision."

"Actually, it's about your prep school." She decided her earlier decision not to bring the subject up no longer applied. Something—or some*one*—had clearly damaged Simon, and this might be her only chance to find out information. "The other night your father mentioned a hazing scandal."

"Oh, that. Yeah, some of the kids on the sports teams got out of hand. Why?"

"After he mentioned it, I read some of the articles and it made me wonder if the same sort of thing went on while you were there."

"Are you kidding?" He gave a short barklike laugh. "Worse."

Blood running cold, she repeated his response, hoping he'd tell her she'd made a mistake. "Worse? How so?"

"Let's just say I'm glad I didn't do football or spring rowing."

Rowing. "Why's that?"

"Well, there was this one kid, Chip Amato, who was a real pig when it came to that stuff. There were all sorts of rumors about what he made kids do down at the boathouse. Nasty things. I'd share, but they're not the sort of thing you talk about in mixed company—if you get my drift."

Delilah did, unfortunately, and she didn't like the picture forming in her mind. "Sounds like a really nice guy."

"Of course they were only rumors, but all the same, where there's smoke…"

"There's fire," she finished for him.

"Exactly."

"And no one said anything? No one told the administrators? The coaches?"

Josh shook his head. "Not while I was there. Seriously, can't blame them for keeping their mouths shut. If some of the stories I heard are true, I wouldn't want to admit what happened, either."

"Suppose not," Delilah murmured. Pieces began sliding into place. Horrible, heartbreaking pieces if the stories Josh heard had any relation to the truth. Poor, poor Simon. She felt sick to her stomach. "Thank you for filling me in."

"No problem. Surprised you asked me instead of Simon though."

"I would have asked him, but he…" She scrambled for an excuse Josh wouldn't question. "He's been preoccupied with impressing your father. I didn't want to bother him with school gossip."

"Fair enough." The chair scraped the cement as he shifted his weight from one foot to another, clearly working up to changing the topic. "By the way…since my role with this agency search is over and I no longer have to take out Roberto's assistant, I was wondering if you and I—"

Delilah could practically hear Simon gloating in her head. *Told you so,* he'd say with that maddeningly attractive smirk. "Josh, you're a really—"

"You don't need to explain," Josh interrupted, thankfully cutting the discussion off before it became any more awkward. "I had a feeling you would say something like that."

"Sorry." He truly was a nice guy. She wished she could make herself be interested.

"You're a terrible liar, you know."

"I'm not lying," she told him. "I really am sorry."

"I believe you. I meant you're lying about nothing going on between you and Simon.

"I saw you on the beach," he added with a crooked smile.

"Then why did you…?" *Oh.* He'd been information fishing. "Your espionage skills improved during the afternoon."

Josh flashed a grin. "What can I say? Practice makes perfect."

Too bad he was still wrong. At least as far as Simon was concerned.

"Bosses often do. You only find out what they're thinking when you mess up." There was a long pause when Delilah didn't reply. Long enough even her mother picked up on it. "Honey, are you sure everything's all right?" she asked.

"Just tired," Delilah assured her. "Smiling all day takes a lot of energy."

"Yes, it does. Hold on, your brother's up." On the other end of the line, she heard her mother cheering.

"Sorry," she said when she returned. "He struck out last time at bat. If he strikes out a second time, Brian will never let him hear the end of it."

"I'll let you get back to cheering him on then," Delilah replied. "I'll call you when I get back to New York."

"And you're sure everything's okay?"

Delilah forced a smile into her voice. "Of course. Everything's great."

No sooner had she hung up than a wave of loneliness struck. There was no one she could share her thoughts with. Not even her best friends, who she thought of as sisters. She liked to think the three of them shared everything, but they didn't, did they? Keeping bad stuff to herself had become such a habit she no longer realized when she was doing it. In fact, the only person she'd come close to sharing with had been Simon. Talk about irony. The two of them were more alike than either realized.

Setting her phone on the nightstand, she stretched out across the paisley comforter and closed her eyes. She must have dozed off because when she opened them, the room was dark. Outside her window, she could see the three-quarter moon hanging above the midnight ocean.

Someone had covered her with a blanket. *Simon.* Awareness flooded her at the notion he had been watching her sleep. Sitting up, she saw her door had been closed, as well. A quick look at the dresser clock told her she'd been asleep a couple of hours.

Outside her door, she heard the floor creak, followed by the soft clap of the screen door being shut. There was only one place she could think of where Simon would head this time of night. A soft splash a few minutes later confirmed her guess.

The tiki torches were still lit, their flames flickering and casting shadows across the concrete surrounding the pool. Now that it was dark, the pool had been lit up and un-

derwater spotlights gave the water an other-
worldly glow.

In the very center, cutting across the surface was Simon, his frame long and lean. His
pace was different. Yesterday, he swam with
an almost manic aggression, his arms at-
tacking the water. Tonight he looked slower,
more… Was it possible to call a swimming
stroke resigned?

Whatever the stroke, his body in motion remained a thing of beauty. Longing filled Delilah's chest. He was too focused to notice her
presence, so she stood by the water's edge and
watched as he completed several more laps.

Eventually, he slowed way down, touched
the wall one last time and stopped. He hov-
ered in the water, his hand on the tiled edge,
the firelight casting shadows on his profile.
Delilah heard the quiet splatter of water mix
with his breathing as he wiped his face.

"Hey," she called out to him.

He turned, and while she knew he was surprised to see her, his expression remained un-
changed. "Hey," he answered back.

"Little late for your morning workout, isn't
it?"

"Swimming helps to clear my head."

"Is it?" she asked. "Clear, that is?"

"Not this time. Maybe in a few more laps."

As though realizing holding their conversation with a pool between them only increased the awkwardness, he swam over to where she stood. Delilah looked down with a smile. "Thank you for the blanket."

"It was nothing."

The air hung thick between them. Simon stood in the chest-high water, his shoulders silver and shadow. Perhaps his swimming closer wasn't such a good idea after all. She felt self-conscious standing over him and looking down.

Ignoring how her skirt would rise up, she rectified the situation by sitting down and slipping her legs into the water. "You were gone a long time. Did you and Bartlett walk all the way to the tip?"

"No, the three of us made camp at the bonfire and talked. Roberto did most of the talking. I decided less was more. Just as well. Turns out I was a bit distracted."

By their conversation on the beach. "You did say you were tired," she said.

"So I did."

They both dodged the obvious. Delilah wondered if he regretted saying anything and waited for the inevitable request for her to forget. To her surprise, none came. Perhaps he realized the list was long enough.

In a way, she wished he *had* spoken. The ensuing silence was way too thick and awkward.

Suddenly, there was a splash and a warm, wet presence filled the space beside her. "I owe you an apology," she heard him say. "It wasn't fair of me to dump my baggage on you. I was tired and spouting a lot of nonsense."

So he was going to skip asking, and go straight to pretending. "Didn't sound like nonsense to me."

"I wish you'd think otherwise."

Too late, she wanted to tell him. The words were already out there.

She settled for kicking her feet back and forth and watching the whirlpools the motion created in the aquamarine depths.

"You didn't come out here to thank me for the blanket, did you?" Simon asked her.

Delilah could lie. She could give him a nice pat answer like she had for the past four years. Only she didn't want to. She'd reached her quota of nice and pat for the weekend. "You want the truth? I was worried about you. Your admission on the beach was pretty rough."

He gave a crooked smile. "Not so rough. I'll survive."

A reassurance that would work better if the smile met his eyes.

"We aren't talking about some embarrassing anecdote, Simon. You called yourself a coward. That's a pretty damning statement."

"Truth isn't always pretty."

"No, it's not." Delilah took a good look at his profile. The shadows under his eyes weren't caused by the light. "Last night, when you talked about the boy not defending himself, you were really talking about yourself, weren't you?"

Simon didn't speak, but the way his body grew taut was answer enough. Hoping the next comment didn't blow up in her face, she plunged on. "I know about the hazing," she said. "About Chip Amato."

Every inch of Simon turned rigid. He pulled himself so tight in fact, she could see the muscles twitch beneath the surface of his skin. "Who told you about Chip?"

"I—" She tucked her hair behind her ear, more to get her nerves under control than anything. "I asked Josh."

"Dammit!" He jumped to his feet, splash-

ing water everywhere as he stalked his way
to a nearby table.

"He didn't say anything specific," she
quickly continued. "Only that there were rumors." Which Simon's agitation gave weight
to. "Whatever happened—"

"Is in the past," Simon spat.

Was it? Delilah might not know the details,
but she wasn't stupid. The scars from whatever happened were still very much present.

She looked at him, standing in the torches'
glow. The night was warm with summer's
heat, yet he was trembling. The uncharacter-
istic fragility broke her heart. Needing to be
closer, she rose and walked toward him, stopping a few inches from his shoulder when he
stiffened. "What happened, Simon?"

"Doesn't matter."

"Maybe not the details, but the pain that
was left behind certainly does."

His eyes had dulled, and she knew his
thoughts had gone to some place inside himself. She stood listening to the sound of his
breathing, not knowing what would happen next. Piece by piece, he'd bury the dark
thoughts until all you could see was his calm,
collected exterior. A mask that told the world
everything was fine.

"I get it," she said. "Wanting to pretend that everything—that you're—okay."

Slowly, he lifted his eyes to look at her. "When my dad died, my mom died, too," she told him. "Only she was still in the house. When she wasn't in bed crying, she was a ghost, walking around the house, barely speaking. For months, I took care of everything, the kids, the house, the bills and…"

She had to sniff back the emotion. After all these years, the memory still hurt. "And the entire time I was afraid if someone found out, they'd come in and take everything away. So when a teacher or people asked how things were at home, I'd put on a big, fake smile and say 'great.' Then, when my mom got better, I kept smiling. I kept saying 'great' even if it wasn't true because who knew what piece of news might send her spiraling back.

"So, I get it," she said. "And I get how it can become second nature, but at some point pretending becomes very lonely." Hand trembling, she reached out to touch his arm. Silently letting him know he didn't have to be alone.

He broke away, back to the pool's edge, where he stood staring into the aqua-colored depths. "You know what I love about swimming?" he asked.

Startled by his change of topic, she didn't answer. He didn't seem to notice because he answered himself. "The peacefulness. When I'm alone doing laps, everything fades away but the sounds of the pool. It's when I can truly be myself."

"You can be yourself now, too," she told him. "I'm not going to judge."

His laugh was soft but skeptical.

When several beats passed, and he didn't say any more, Delilah's hope for an explanation faded. It was foolish of her to think he'd open up to her in the first place. It was obvious he regretted what little he did say. If only he would trust her, she thought sadly.

"I didn't fight."

"What?" She'd turned to walk away and barely heard his softly spoken words.

"I said I didn't fight." His eyes were hard and glittering. "They found me in the boathouse and I should have fought them, and I didn't."

"Them?" She hadn't stopped to think, but of course, Chip would bring his teammates. "How many were there?"

"Why does it matter?"

"Because—"

He whirled around. "Didn't you hear what I said? I didn't fight. Instead I cried, and I let them pin my arms, and I did what they told me to do. Like a pathetic coward."

Dear God. She pressed her hand to her mouth to keep from crying out loud. The tears burned her eyes anyway. Poor, poor Simon. "You were fifteen years old and outnumbered. You weren't—"

"Don't tell me what I wasn't!" he hissed. "For God's sake, I gave in without a fight. If that doesn't tell you what kind of man I really am, I don't know what does."

As he ran a hand through his wet curls, his face caught the light, and for the first time Delilah could see how heavily his thoughts weighed on him.

How many times had she looked at this same profile and felt her heart skip a beat? Tonight, she saw a different man. One who was vulnerable and damaged and that same heart ached like never before. The emotions inside her shifted. Infatuation became something far deeper.

Slowly, she walked toward him and without a word or a second thought, wrapped her arms around him. His body stiffened and his fingers gripped her shoulders to push her away, but she held firm.

"I'm sorry," she whispered in his ear. "So, so sorry."

She heard a hitch in his breath as a tremor passed through his body. Another shudder, and he drew her close, burying his face in the crook of her neck. Moved by the unexpected show of vulnerability, Delilah carded her fingers in his curls and pressed soft kisses to his temple. Just thinking about the injustice brought tears to her eyes. Squeezing her eyes shut, she let the moisture slide down her cheeks. She held him tight, offering solace. For what Simon had endured and for the shame he needlessly felt. And for all those years of feeling alone with no one to talk to.

Eventually, Simon's breathing slowed. His grip, which had been like steel, loosened as his hands began to stroke a path up and down her spine. Slowly other things made their way into Delilah's consciousness. Things like the way his damp body molded against hers. There was a growing pressure against her hip bone. Without thinking, Delilah shifted her hips. The movement earned her a groan, and told her she wasn't the only one becoming flooded with awareness.

She opened her eyes to find Simon looking down on her, his eyes blown wide with desire. Delilah's eyes fluttered closed as his caress traveled down her temple and along to her cheekbone before finally coming to a stop on her lips, where they lightly ran back and forth across her Cupid's bow. This time it was her breath that hitched. Her eyes opened. Simon was still staring at her, the desire in his eyes more inflamed than ever. He seemed to be waiting for permission before moving forward. Delilah parted her lips in answer.

His kiss was hard and desperate. Delilah clung to his shoulders. Four years of desire sprung free and she kissed him back with every ounce of her being. Pool water dampened her dress, turning the thin material into cream-and-yellow tracing paper, but she didn't care. Just so long as Simon kept kissing her.

When they finally broke for air, their ragged breath drowned out all other sounds. Simon looked as dazed as she felt. "Delilah," he gasped. "I want…"

"Yes," she replied. There was no need for him to finish the question. They both wanted. "Yes."

Slipping her hand in his, she let him lead her back to the cottage.

CHAPTER EIGHT

"I'M SORRY ABOUT your mother."

It was later. Simon sat in an oversized easy chair looking out at the ocean.

Delilah—curled in his lap—shrugged, her shoulder rubbing against his bare skin. "Me too," she said. A familiar-sounding resignation laced her words. Sad to think they shared such a sad bond. "She always said my father was her missing piece."

"Her what?"

She tilted her head back revealing a face sleepy and too adorable not to kiss. "Missing piece," she repeated. "Like a puzzle nine hundred and ninety-nine one-thousandths complete. You need that one thousandth piece to finish the picture."

"I see."

"Anyway—" her head fell back against his

shoulder "—I guess when he died, the hole he left behind felt too big."

Simon's chest hurt. It wasn't right that she had to deal with such a heavy burden so young. For four years, he saw Delilah as an overwhelmingly competent and reliable employee. Now he knew the source of her reliability. Not to mention that there was a whole lot of passion lurking underneath, he added with a smile.

Hopefully her mother appreciated having such a strong daughter in her corner. "She's better now, right?" he asked.

"Better. Not 100 percent, but better." With a delicate yawn, she nestled closer. "Though I suppose when you lose your soul mate, you can't ever go back to 100 percent, can you?"

"I wouldn't know. I never lost a soul mate." Soul mates weren't a concept he ever considered. With as many pieces as he had missing, he doubted there was anyone who fit.

"Me neither. But like my mother says, every puzzle has its piece, every pot has a lid. You just have to find it."

Her sentence faded in a sleepy slur. Reaching behind him, Simon grabbed the throw off the bed and draped it over their bodies. "Go to sleep," he whispered. "I'll tuck you in."

The conversation left him with an odd disquiet. He didn't want to think about pieces or lids or anything else that would kill his mood. Tonight was the first time he could remember feeling peaceful outside the water. He wanted to savor the moment for as long as possible.

Somewhere around dawn, he suspected he'd developed an addiction as he couldn't get enough. Delilah's scent, her taste—hell, every little sound she made—might as well have been drugs. Seeing her laid out beneath him, made him feel stronger than he thought possible. An hour couldn't go by before the need to lose himself inside her gripped him again. He went to pull her warm, willing body to his only to swipe empty sheets.

What the...? "Delilah?"

She wasn't in the room. Rolling on to his back, Simon blinked at the white ceiling. Maybe she went across the hall to try and sleep. Should he go check or would that look too needy? A hollow feeling he couldn't decipher had lodged itself in his chest. Truncated arousal, probably, or bruised ego. He wasn't used to a woman who wasn't there when he reached for her.

It was a good thing, he decided, her ducking out. Gave him time to clear his head. In the dark, he'd managed to avoid dealing with his humiliating breakdown, but now, without Delilah's presence to distract him—or sex to distract her from asking further questions— the details came flying back. Lord knew what she thought of him now.

He closed his eyes and tried to imagine the water, forcing Atlantic navy to replace hypnotic blue eyes. The damage had been done. Best he could do now was to start fresh. Act as though he'd never fallen apart, that he'd never said anything about the boathouse. After all, wasn't pretending his best skill?

The door opened, and Delilah walked in carrying two cups of coffee. Simon waited until she set one down on the nightstand before saying good morning.

"Oh!" She started, coffee sloshing over the rim of her mug. "You're awake."

"And you got dressed." In black pants and a businesslike blouse to boot. Between the clothes and the coffee, they might as well be back at the office.

"Um, yes." Running a hand around her ear, she seemed suddenly fascinated with the contents of her cup. "I didn't think the Bartletts would want to see me walking around in my nightgown. Or last night's wrinkled dress," she added, her eyes disappearing behind her mug. Hard to tell in the sunlight, but Simon thought her skin looked suspiciously pink.

"Who said you had to walk around at all?" he asked.

She ignored his not-so-subtle hint, choosing instead to pace toward the back window. "I went to get coffee. You, I mean *we,* didn't get much sleep last night…"

"Is that a complaint?"

"What? No, not at all. Last night was… wonderful." This time her skin definitely turned pink. "I just thought you might want some caffeine before your meeting."

Meeting? Dammit, that's right. Bartlett wanted them all to enjoy breakfast together before heading out. "Another round of socializing for dollars." With a long breath, he fell back against the pillow.

"Is that going to be a problem?" She headed back to the bed. "I can make some sort of excuse if you're not feeling up to it."

"You don't need to make up anything. I'm not some fragile creature that needs protecting."

"I know that."

Did she? Because despite his pretense, his

confession apparently loomed large. Last night's comfort was quickly receding.

Not ready for reality to return, he held out a hand. "Come here." When she moved close enough, he took the coffee cup from her before running his fingers down the front of her shirt. "Did I ever tell you how much I hate black pants?"

"You do?"

"Yep." Hooking his finger into her waistband, he tugged her closer. The tiny gasp as she tumbled onto the bed made him hot all over. "Right now, I hate them very, very much." He buried his head in the crook of her neck, earning himself another sigh.

"What about the breakfast meeting?"

"Let them wait. It'll give Roberto more time to talk himself out of an account. Right now, we have more important things to focus on." While he was speaking, he slipped the ponytail holder from her hair, letting the strands fall like a brown silk curtain. Fingers twisting in the softness, he sought her mouth.

"Simon…"

"Shhh," he murmured against her lips. He was back in control now. And he was going to make her forget the man she met last night ever existed.

* * *

Sixty minutes later, Simon escorted Delilah poolside. Bartlett, it turned out, hadn't even appeared yet. "Too bad we didn't look out the window," he whispered. "We could have lingered a little longer over coffee."

"Your coffee got cold," she whispered back.

"Really? Seemed hot enough to me." Her mouth made that cute little goldfish movement. Before she could find her words, he slipped his top smile into place. "Good morning," he greeted Josh, his voice probably more boisterous than necessary. "Everyone up and ready to conquer the day?"

"Yes," Josh replied. "Looks like my father's turned everyone into early risers."

"Why not? You can learn a lot about a man by how he handles the morning after a night's indulgence, right?"

No sooner did Simon speak than Jim Bartlett came strolling around the main house. Simon swore the man listened and waited for the best entrance moment. "You make me sound so calculating, Cartwright."

"Just a man who knows how he wants things done," Simon replied. "Besides, we're all businessmen here. After seventy-two hours together, we might as well call a spade a spade, don't you think?"

"Quite right. I appreciate the honesty." Clapping Simon on the shoulder, he turned his attention to Delilah and Carl. "And I appreciate the two of you getting up early, as well. I trust everyone slept well?"

Simon suppressed a smile as Delilah grabbed for her cup. "Very well thank you," she said from behind the rim.

"Good. Good. I thought I heard a couple people in the pool last night. Was that you and Simon?"

"I."

She looked in Simon's direction, and he immediately jumped in. "We took a quick swim," he said, insides tense. He had been so focused on Delilah forgetting his meltdown, he failed to realize others might have also heard. His stomach dropped. "I hope we didn't make too much noise."

Bartlett waved his hand. "If you only knew how many late-night rendezvous have taken place in that pool."

"I wouldn't exactly call it a rendezvous," Delilah said, coffee-cup-turned-shield firmly in place.

"Rendezvous, midnight swim. Point is, you didn't keep me up."

"I didn't hear anything, either," Roberto added, "but then I was so full from yesterday's dinner I fell asleep the minute I hit the pillow."

His remark turned the conversation back to yesterday's party. Relieved, Simon sat back, content to let Roberto do most of the talking. His rival had a tendency to go overboard with the compliments. A poor strategy when dealing with a man like Bartlett who, Simon suspected, preferred bluntness. At least when it came to other people.

A few feet away, Delilah sipped her coffee in similar silence. Every so often, she'd smile or offer a soft laugh. Every time she did, a series of flutter kicks would go off in his stomach. How quickly an impression could change. Seventy-two hours ago he would have stupidly insisted his assistant blended into the scenery. Now he wondered how the rest of the table could concentrate. Simple things like the way her lips curled up mesmerized him. Catching her eye, he winked. For a moment, her smile brightened in his direction.

She looked so at home in this environment. In his mind's eye, he could easily see her in a house very much like this one. Sitting by the pool with her coffee. Wearing a discarded shirt from the night before. It made a very pleasing picture.

A very permanent kind of picture. One fitting a very permanent kind of woman.

Son-of-a... His coffee cup rattled the glass tabletop. What had he done? In his desperation to forget, he'd slept with the very type of woman he swore he'd never go near—a woman with substance.

Last night's pillow talk flooded back in a rush, dragging along all the disquiet he'd been too sated to acknowledge. Soul mates, lids, puzzle pieces. No way would she indulge in a short-term fling. A woman like Delilah expected more. She *deserved* more.

What she didn't deserve was a pretend shell of a man.

And what did he do? Used her in the worst possible way, tainting the best relationship he would ever have.

Just when he didn't think it was possible to loathe his true nature any more, he'd outdone himself.

"Simon, what is it?" Delilah whispered, trying not to attract the attention of anyone else at the table.

Simon's face had gone suddenly white. Hating that she couldn't reach across the table to comfort him, Delilah played back the conversation to remember what might have been said to provoke the change. Nothing. "Are you all right?"

He flashed a flawless smile. "Don't be silly. Everything's fine."

The lie made her heart sink. He was performing again. Having seen both sides, she knew the difference better than ever. Last night's Simon was nowhere in sight. She'd never know he'd been there at all except for her memories. She wanted to blame the added company for the shift. After all, he couldn't very well canoodle with her over French toast in front of a prospective client and a colleague.

There was only one problem with her theory—the shift had started before breakfast. There'd been a distance when they'd made love this morning that hadn't been there last night.

If she were to be brutally honest, she held part of the blame. Last night had been... She couldn't come up with words. All these years nursing a fantasy and reality blew those dreams out of the water. Simon and she connected in a way that went far beyond comfort or sex. She knew now what she'd been feeling all those years was mere infatuation. Last night was about love. Deep, lasting love.

The feeling scared her to death. Finally, she understood what her mother felt. What it meant to find the person who filled the empty spot in your soul. Simon just had to whisper her name and she melted. It was all too good to be true. Too much to believe.

And now she was frightened by the distress in Simon's eyes. What if he didn't feel the same? What then? She didn't want to contemplate the emptiness.

An eternity later, breakfast finally ended. Delilah said her goodbyes and headed back to the guest cottage. Hopefully once she and Simon were alone, and he let his guard back down, her insecurity would go away.

Unfortunately, no sooner did they cross the threshold than Jim came jogging across the stone patio.

"I was wondering if you might hang out a little longer," he said. "Come up to the main house and chat. There were a couple of topics we touched on last night I'd like to get your input on in greater depth."

"Of course," Simon replied. "I'll be up shortly."

"Take your time," the older man said. "Maybe walk up in twenty minutes or so?"

"Isn't Roberto's car coming to get him in twenty minutes?" Delilah asked once the door was shut.

Simon wore a neutral expression, one she'd seen dozens of times, right after he scored a major account victory. "Now that you mention it, Roberto did say something to that effect."

Meaning if Bartlett hadn't chosen CMT, he was pretty darn close. Thrilled for him, Delilah launched herself into his arms. "Congratulations!"

The return embrace didn't materialize. "Let's not celebrate prematurely," he said, untangling himself. "He could simply have more questions."

"Only he said input. That implies he wants your opinion, and if he wants to wait until after the Mediatopia representatives are gone...." It seemed to her the implication was obvious. Any other time, Simon would at least acknowledge the possibility. Why was he so hesitant now?

"I don't want to get ahead of myself, is all," he told her when she asked. "This account is too important. Until Bartlett's signature is on the contract, I'm not going to make any assumptions."

"Fine. You can be cautious. I'll be optimistic and plan on celebrating on the flight back to New York."

"About that…" He rubbed the back of his neck. The hair on Delilah's prickled. "I was thinking you should go ahead and fly home without me."

"You want me to leave?" She tried to ignore her growing apprehension

"We don't know how long this meeting will take. Bartlett could keep me here all afternoon."

Me, not *we.* Until that moment they'd been a team. "I don't mind staying," she replied.

Meanwhile, Simon was making a point of walking around the cottage, studying everything but her.

"I don't want you wasting your whole afternoon," he said, his hand finding its way to his neck again. "I've already ruined…" She saw him wince, the expression matching the catch in her chest. "This trip's already eaten up enough of your weekend," he started over. "I'm sure you've got things you need to do."

It couldn't be. He was giving her the brush-off. She wasn't any different than Finland Smythe.

No wonder this morning seemed off. He wasn't making love to her; he was saying goodbye.

God, what an idiot. Thinking there'd been some kind of deep, mutual connection. She could kick herself.

As if the humiliation wasn't complete, practical matters worked their way into her head. His send-off wasn't as neat as he'd like it to be. "There's one problem," she said, moving so he had to face her. "We drove here together. How are we supposed to go to the airport at different times if we have one car?"

"You can take the car. I'm sure Jim or Josh will be glad to drive me back."

She'd hoped he'd use her point as an excuse to keep her around. She was wrong. "Looks like you've thought of everything," she murmured.

"Surprising, I know, but every once in a while I manage to function without an assistant doing the work for me." Cupping the back of her neck, he kissed her, stopping just short of letting the passion build. Delilah clung to his arms in spite of herself.

"I'll see you back in New York, okay?" he said, smiling.

No, it wasn't okay, she wanted to scream. Because she didn't want to go. Because she couldn't have imagined last night's connection.

Because the smile he gave her was the same blindingly charming smile he gave the rest of the world.

She forced a giant smile of her own. "Sure," she told him. "That sounds great."

"Sorry I'm late." With her mane of curls looking wilder than usual, Chloe rushed through the front door and plopped down into the booth. "Mmm, breakfast for dinner. My favorite combination."

Delilah eyed her friend's large green-and-white cup. "Long line at the coffee shop?" Even if she hadn't dragged a latte into the diner with her, Chloe's makeup would have given her away.

Her friend ducked her head. "I can't help myself. He's everything I like in a guy. Good-looking, creative, nonconforming..."

"Unreliable, uninterested."

"I wouldn't say completely uninterested. He gave me a free upgrade this morning, and extra foam. I like to think it's because I'm special," she added, saluting the air with her cup.

"You do know you're crazy, right?" *Like she could judge.* Chloe's barista crush was no worse than Delilah falling for her boss. In fact, it was better since Chloe's heart wasn't so deeply involved.

The waitress came over, saw Chloe's cup and gave them both glares before asking Chloe if she planned to eat.

"And as usual, you made a friend, too," Delilah remarked after the waitress departed.

"Wow. I thought being snarky was my job. What happened? Bad business trip? I've got to admit, I wasn't expecting to see you until tomorrow."

"I caught an earlier shuttle." *Per Simon's request,* she added bitterly to herself.

In the end, Josh drove her to Logan, shooting her strange looks the entire way. Clearly he didn't buy Simon's excuse about wasting the day any more than she did.

"An earlier shuttle, huh? That doesn't sound good. Does this mean no Bartlett account?" Chloe asked.

"Actually, Simon stayed behind because Bartlett wanted to meet privately. The invitation sounded very positive. I won't be surprised if we get a big thumbs-up next week."

"Really? Why are you so out of sorts then? Seriously, Delilah, you look like someone killed your best friend, and since I'm still breathing, and I managed not to kill Larissa at the bridal expo yesterday...."

"Bad?"

"You don't know the half of it. There had to be two thousand women at that expo and at least half of them were as wedding crazy as our La-Roo. Do you know I almost had to break up a fight between her and some other bride over color swatches? *Color swatches!* Our friend has officially crossed over into Bridezilla territory."

"Maybe we'll get lucky and Tom will pull her back."

"Doubt it. He's less interested than my barista. La-Roo's going all wedding crazy, and he just lets her."

"He wants her to be happy, that's all."

"Maybe," her friend said, her frown suggesting otherwise. "Right now, though, I'd rather talk about you being happy. You didn't answer my question, by the way."

"What question?"

She was dodging, and both of them knew it.

While the waitress's return kept Chloe from responding right away, Delilah knew the reprieve wouldn't last. As soon as their omelets were served, her friend would be right back on point.

"Did something happen? Because like I said, you don't look like a woman returning from a successful business trip. And," she commented, brandishing a forkful of egg white, "don't tell me you're feeling tired. I've seen you pull all-nighters and be in a better mood."

Delilah stared at her meal. "It's complicated," she said, borrowing one of Simon's favorite phrases. "I'm not sure where to start."

"The beginning works for me."

"I do that, and we'll be here all night."

"Good thing this place has twenty-four-hour service then."

Delilah smiled. Things would be so much easier if she could simply pretend like always. Only she couldn't anymore; she was too confused, and too tired of dealing with things alone. Talking with Simon last night showed her what connection could feel like.

"Have you ever thought you'd found your soul mate only to start wondering later on if you've made a mistake?"

"You're kidding, right?" Chloe asked, laughing. "This is me you're talking to. Picking the wrong man is generational in my family." Her smile faded. "You met someone in Boston?"

"Sort of."

"Get out!" Her friend slapped the table, drawing anther glare from the waitress. "Delilah St. Germain had a fling. Now you're having buyer's remorse, is that it?"

Delilah's cheeks grew warm at the blunt description. "I didn't consider it a fling at the time."

"We never do. Unfortunately, in my opinion, most men think otherwise. I take it you really liked this guy?"

"And I thought after he…" That's what hurt the most. Last night, when Simon opened up, she'd felt so close to him only for him to turn around and shut her out again. "I thought we had a connection."

"Connections only work for phone companies."

"Little harsh, don't you think?"

"Is it? Lord knows, I've yet to see any instant attraction pan out."

Delilah didn't bother arguing the point. Instead, she chose to focus on her half-eaten omelet, poking holes in the surface with her fork and watching the cheese bubble out. "My parents fell in love at first sight," she said in a soft voice. "My mom never loved anyone else."

"Really? Wow. That's actually…"

"Lame?"

"Amazing-sounding."

"Yeah it is, isn't it?" Delilah agreed. Which was part of the problem. Growing up in the shadow of a fairy tale made all her other relationships that much more difficult.

"So you think this guy from Boston was love at first sight?"

Delilah thought back to her very first day when Simon walked into her life. "I thought so, but I'm beginning to realize what I thought was love was really infatuation. The more I got to know the real him, however, the harder I fell."

"Wait a minute." Chloe frowned. "I thought you met this man while you were away."

"Told you this was complicated."

"All right, now you have to start at the beginning. What's this man's name?"

Afraid to look her friend in the eye, Delilah continued poking holes. "Simon Cartwright."

"Our boss?"

Delilah nodded.

Chloe sat back, her face the picture of disbelief. "Tell me you're kidding."

"Wish I was."

"I can't believe.... For how long? I mean, how long have you had a thing for him?"

"Four years."

"Since orientation?"

"Afraid so."

All of a sudden a piece of fried potato smacked her in the face. Looking up, Delilah met Chloe's brown glare. "Four freaking years and you didn't tell us? What gives? I thought we told each other everything."

At the sound of her friend's hurt voice, Delilah cringed. Chloe had every right to be angry. She *had* held back. "I guess I was afraid."

"Afraid of what?"

"The truth blowing up in my face." She thought about all the years she had protected her mother. "I guess I've gotten used to keeping a part of me locked away," she said. "It's easier to deal with thoughts in my head than say them out loud and deal with the fallout."

"You should know we'd never judge you, no matter what the thought."

"I know. I'm sorry I never said anything."

Chloe reached over and covered her hand. "You didn't do anything I haven't done myself. Other than fall for our boss, that is. Even I'm not that crazy. But the stuff about you keeping everything inside? That's old news, my friend."

"It is?" *How?*

"You don't think La-Roo and I didn't notice you never have problems while we complain about everything?" Chloe explained. "We always figured if a problem got big enough you'd let us know."

A lump rose in Delilah's throat. She'd never realized. Looks like she finally had a problem big enough. "Thank you," she whispered.

"We're friends, Del. We'll be here for you no matter what. Although, you do know I'm going to have to tell Larissa about this, and we'll probably talk about you behind your back."

Delilah's smiled despite her watery vision. "Of course. What are friends for?"

"You also know that I'll be compelled to mock Simon now every time his photo's in the paper."

"You do already."

"I mean mock more."

"Okay." What little appetite she'd had disappeared, and she pushed her plate aside. "I can't believe I made such a stupid mistake."

"We can't help who we fall for. Take it from someone who knows."

Maybe not, but she could help acting like a lovesick fool. Simon didn't have relationships that lasted longer than a couple of weeks. What made her think she would be any different?

Needing something to keep her hands busy, she plucked a sugar packet from the holder and ground the paper between her fingers. The grains slid back and forth, sharp and rough.

"I think I'm in love with him, Chloe."

Correction. She *knew.* She fell hard and for real at the pool Saturday night.

"Does Simon know how you feel?"

"Does it matter?"

"I think it does. I mean..." Her friend sat back and appeared to seriously think about her words. "This isn't like my thing for the barista. You're not the type of person who throws the word *love* around easily. If you're saying it out loud, I'm going to guess you've got good reason. There must be some kind of emotional connection between the two of you."

A connection? She'd held him while he shook, witnessed him letting his guard down. Was that because there was a bond or had she simply been convenient?

So many questions and so few answers. Maybe coming back early was a good thing, after all. Gave her space and time to think things through.

"If you'd asked me last night, I would have told you yes. This morning, I'm not so sure." She tossed the sugar packet aside. "At least I'm not so sure it goes both ways." When it came to Simon, she wasn't sure of anything.

"Have you asked him?"

"No." Like always, she'd been too worried about the fallout to do anything but pretend.

"Well, I'm no relationship expert, but I'd say talking to him would be the first step. Who knows, maybe you'll be the woman to unseat Finland Smythe."

"They broke up last week," Delilah told her.

"Oh, for crying out loud, why am I always the last to find these things out? Seriously though, I might not be a big believer in soul mates and fate and all that, but that doesn't mean I wouldn't like to see my friends prove me wrong."

She looked Delilah in the eye. "You deserve to be loved back."

The lump Delilah had been battling in her throat returned, larger than ever, making her eyes water. "You, too," she whispered, giving her friend a watery smile.

"That's what friends are for," Chloe replied, her brown eyes shining, as well. "By the way, for what it's worth, Cartwright doesn't know what he's missing."

For the first time all day, Delilah didn't feel so alone. She reached over and gave Chloe's hand a squeeze. "Neither does the barista."

CHAPTER NINE

"NICE SKIRT."

The receptionist's compliment caught Delilah off guard. Were her clothes that predictable? She could almost hear Chloe and Larissa saying *yes*. Then again, she was the one who picked the pink tiered skirt this morning instead of pants. In the back of her mind, she had this crazy notion that changing up her wardrobe might make today go her way. After all, she'd been wearing a dress the first time Simon opened up to her. Maybe seeing her legs would inspire him to open up again.

The young woman handed her the daily sign-in sheet. "Wow, this is a first," she said. "I don't think you've ever arrived after Mr. Cartwright before."

What? "Simon's already here?"

"Uh-huh. Showed up a half hour ago."

Sure enough, his heavy black scrawl topped

the list. Terrific. The one day she needed time to compose herself was the one day he decided to skip the pool.

"Did he say why he was here so early?"

"No, but he was in a mood. Barely said two words."

And he usually he made a point of greeting everyone. Not good.

Of course, she reminded herself, his mood could very well have nothing to do with this weekend. That didn't stop her stomach from churning during the elevator ride.

She, Chloe and, later, Larissa had spent a good chunk of the evening talking about what happened on Saturday night. But while she loved her newly discovered support, there was still one secret she didn't share: Simon's history. She'd lost sight of his traumatic confession in the haze of lovemaking. Looking back over the night, she wondered if the distraction wasn't on purpose. Simon would naturally want to bury the unpleasant memories again. Out of sight, out of mind—wasn't that his motto? Meanwhile she'd been too spellbound to think clearly.

She wasn't stupid though. She knew that one admission, no matter how difficult to make, wouldn't erase the scars.

A swear word spit from her lips, loud in the empty space. Every time she thought of what happened, she wanted to scream. Those boys took so much from Simon. They took his dignity, his innocence, and for what? Some stupid team prank? How many other boys suffered the same violation? How many suffered and didn't have the strength Simon had to rise above the trauma? Then again, she wasn't sure Simon realized how much strength he had. Certainly didn't seem to, based on the comments he made.

His doubt was what made her the most apprehensive.

The elevator doors opened and she found herself entering chaos. A half dozen employees were already scrambling, many still wearing their suit jackets. That never happened during hot summer months. Managers were sitting in cubicles rather than in their offices.

Simon sat at the creative administrator's desk with a phone tucked under his ear. As soon as Delilah saw him, her heart took a tumble. He had his jacket off. The sleeves of his white shirt were rolled back, showing off his tanned forearms. It was her favorite look for him. It showed him as a man in his element.

She waited until Simon finished his conversation, before giving a small cough to get his attention. He looked up. Their eyes locked, and Delilah watched a series of emotions play out. Embarrassment, sadness and something else. She wanted to say regret, but it flashed by too quickly for her to say for certain.

"Good," he said. "You're here."

The receptionist was right; he wasn't smiling. He had the intense look of focus he got whenever there was a crisis.

Before she could blink, Simon headed down the hall toward his office, forcing her to hurry to catch up. "What's going on?"

"Evidently my father, as well as a couple other board members, had dinner with the mayor last night and pledged *pro bono* support for city hall's new witness intimidation campaign."

"That's a good thing, isn't it?" A successful campaign would give CMT a lot of visibility.

"They want the campaign to coincide with the Martin Santiago trial."

Delilah nearly stumbled on her heels. "They what?"

Martin Santiago was a high school honor student who'd been shot while buying fruit at a corner market. Despite the fact the crime occurred in broad daylight, the police had a hard time making an arrest, largely because the suspects, two well-known gang members, had intimidated witnesses. Timing-wise, the high-profile trial was the perfect time to launch a new initiative. There was only one problem.

"Didn't I read in the paper they were picking jurors this week?"

"Yep. Which means we've got forty-eight hours to create and implement the campaign."

"Holy smoke." All the craziness began to make sense. Simon's father didn't just volunteer the agency's services, he volunteered them for a Herculean task.

"A couple people from the mayor's office are on their way over right now to give us more details. We'll meet with them, then we'll brainstorm with the creative team.

"This is going to be an all-hands-on-deck kind of day," he said. "Everything else has to take a backseat."

Everything else meaning their personal situation. He no doubt welcomed the situation.

They reached his office at the same time their discussion ended. Without work to talk about, they were left standing in awkward silence. So different from Saturday night when whispers and touches flowed freely.

"How did your meeting with Bartlett go?" she finally asked.

"Good. Promising. I think we're his first choice."

Dear God, he sounded so businesslike he might as well cut her off at the knees. "That's wonderful. You must be pleased."

"Like I said yesterday, I don't want to get ahead of myself. If there's nothing else, I've got a few phone calls to make."

Delilah noticed his hand resting on the doorknob, ready to close her out. *Not yet.* Trembling, she covered his fingers with her own.

Time ticked slower while she waited for him to react. He didn't speak. But he didn't move his hand away, either. Finally, he turned in her direction. His tortured eyes found hers, and for a few seconds the connection they forged in Massachusetts burned strong.

Until he slowly pushed the door open, letting her touch slip away. "I have a team of city hall consultants coming in less than five minutes expecting brilliance," he said. "I really need to get those calls made."

"Go ahead," she told him. "I'm not going anywhere."

He'd botched that conversation rather nicely, hadn't he?

Did you really think it would go well? Simon ran a hand along the back of his neck. Ninety hours later and he still had the damn headache. Only now a throbbing empty hole in his chest had decided to join in. Being back in New York was supposed to make him feel better. Instead, he felt worse than ever.

And he knew why, too. Nothing like two waves of thought crashing in his head. Now, along with replaying that morning in the boathouse, he had the pleasure of remembering Saturday night, as well. Along with Friday afternoon. And Thursday night. And just about every moment he spent in Delilah's company. How she tasted, how she smelled. How good he felt holding her in his arms.

I'm not going anywhere. That's what he was afraid of. Although if she did leave, he didn't know what he'd do.

Oh, for crying out loud, why couldn't he simply tell her Saturday was a mistake and get it over with? *Once a coward, always a coward, right, Cartwright?* Honestly, he'd never had trouble breaking things off with women before. But, as this weekend seemed to hammer home, Delilah wasn't like other women.

What killed him most of all was that for all these years he'd believed himself to be dead inside as well as broken. Turns out life had one more cruel joke to play. As Saturday night had proved, he was very much alive.

Still, breaking off things was the right thing to do. He needed to cast Delilah loose before she got too attached. Let her go so she could find a man who was worthy.

There was a knock, and Delilah returned carrying a coffee and taunting him with a tight pink skirt. "The people from the mayor's office are here. Would you like me to stay?"

Talk about a double-edged question. He pretended to study the paper in front of him so she couldn't see his reaction. "Please."

The mayor's people arrived, and the next eight hours passed in a whirl of politics, brainstorming and more politics. They decided on a combination of subway and bus posters, internet ads and an aggressive social media campaign—a challenge given the tight turn-around, but he assured his mayorship they'd get the job done. Now all that remained was getting copy that all parties agreed on. He was getting a crash course on the grinding wheels of bureaucracy.

"Creative emailed the latest version of the bus ads." Delilah walked in and dropped a stack of printed pages on his desk.

Picking up the top page, Simon studied it while rubbing the back of his neck. "Did it go to everyone who needs to sign off this time?"

"Every one of them. Fingers crossed that the tenth time's a charm."

He dropped the page. "Do *not* tell me you sent the tenth version. We're on twelve."

"Figure of speech," she snapped.

"My mistake."

They were both tired and short-tempered. Working shoulder to shoulder all day long didn't help. Every time she leaned close, his body went on full alert.

Then there was the fact she was behaving exactly as he wanted her to—professional and distant. It made every movement, every look, every nuance worse.

Giving his neck another rub, he made a point of softening his tone. "What's the deal with the internet copy?"

"Good news there. Everyone at City Hall has signed off. Pending minor changes, that is. They've decided to reinsert the comma."

After taking the mark out two rounds earlier. "Thank God it wasn't a semicolon or we'd still be arguing."

"On the plus side…" He practically crumpled the document he held the paper so tight. Delilah had moved around to his side of the desk to mark a page. Her skin smelled of talcum powder, sweet and clean.

"Is something wrong?" she asked.

What was wrong is that she was driving him insane.

Pushing his chair back a few inches, he began again. "The mayor's communications director said she was very impressed with our ability to turn this sucker around. Meaning there's probably going to be a lot more pro bono projects in our future."

"Is that a good thing or a bad thing?"

"Depends on how you look at it. If you like dropping everything and dealing with the wheels of bureaucracy, it's excellent."

"Guess I should make a note to stock up on pain relievers and antacids," she replied dryly.

The phone rang. Before Simon could say a word, Delilah answered. "Jim Bartlett," she said, handing him the phone. "Says he has some good news for you."

At least something went right this weekend.

It was an effort not to let their hands touch as she handed him the phone, but Delilah managed to do so. All this closeness was driving her insane. How on earth was she supposed to pretend as though there was nothing between them when every time she brought in a new batch of paperwork, she found herself tempted to touch him?

Naturally, they worked well together. Even in awkwardness, their natural communication rose to the surface. Come to think of it, maybe the exceptional teamwork was causing her frustration. Making love to Simon had opened her eyes to how good they could be outside the office and making her wonder if working together could ever be enough for her again.

Her biggest fear was that Simon might think differently. Until they talked about Saturday night, she wouldn't know. And thus far, Simon seemed determined not to talk.

A few feet away Simon said his goodbyes. "You can finally say congratulations," he said upon hanging up. "We have officially been named the agency of record for Bartlett Breweries."

"Congratulations." The first genuine smile she'd had all day found its way to her face. She was happy for Simon, and for the agency. "I knew you would impress them."

He gave her a long, appreciative look that melted her in a way no seductive glance ever could. "You never lost faith, did you?"

"I've seen you in action, remember?"

"Right, my charming self."

The conversation was veering a little too close to the one they weren't supposed to be having. Much as she longed to stay on the track, Delilah allowed him to escape by changing the topic. She smiled her second real smile. "You don't seem very excited for a man who got good news," she told him.

"I'm tired is all. Plus, in the end, it's really just another account, albeit a vital one. Don't tell Bartlett I said that though."

"My lips are sealed. You going to tell the board the good news?"

"Later. Once this project is over. I don't have time for them right now."

His response brought her third real smile of the day. "You're making them wait because they dumped this project on us last-minute, aren't you?"

"Damn straight."

At some point during their conversation, he'd pulled his chair back to its original position. Their bodies were practically touching. Less than an inch separated her knee from his hand. Simon must have noticed too because he'd gone back to studying the paper he crumpled earlier.

Studying him, Delilah saw the bone-deep fatigue lining his face. It took willpower, but she kept herself from brushing his cheek, even though her heart wanted to do nothing more. "No offense," she said, "but you look terrible."

"Headaches will do that to you."

"You've had a lot of headaches the past four days."

"It's been a long four days."

"So it has," she agreed sadly.

He looked up, and once again appreciation shone in his eyes. "Turns out I owe you an apology."

"For what?"

"Sniping at you about the boat ride. You were right, Tom's and Louisa's opinions do carry a ton of weight, and they adored you.

Made my job a whole lot easier, that's for certain."

"Well, my job is to make your job easier. Or did you forget our conversation?"

"I remember," he answered. Heat flashed behind the blue. "I remember everything about Sunday morning."

His voice dropped. "I remember the whole weekend."

"So do I," Delilah replied. The desire she caught in his stare gave her hope. He wanted her. That had to mean *something,* didn't it?

To hell with it. She was done pretending. Playing as though she didn't feel the emotions churning inside her. Either Simon wanted her or didn't want her. She needed to know.

He was doing everything he could to avoid looking at her. Refusing to look away, she brushed his cheek. The shadowed, rough skin scraped her fingertips. "Simon," she started.

"Delilah, please..."

His argument weakened when he let the sentence fade into nothingness. Cupping his cheek, she lifted his face until she could see his eyes. Dear Lord, but they were so blue and so filled with hunger.

Yeah, he wanted her.

She leaned in and kissed him.

In a flash, Simon's arms were around her. *I knew it!* She silently cheered. She knew she hadn't imagined the connection tying them together. She felt the evidence in every kiss, received confirmation from every touch.

His hands pulled her closer.

Despite his conscience screaming at him, any sense of resolve Simon had disappeared the second Delilah's lips touched his. This afternoon's torture had gone on too long. When she touched his cheek, he was lost. Cupping her neck he pulled her close, moaning at how easily she tumbled into him.

Knowing the passion they were capable of sharing, he didn't waste time with gentle coaxing or seduction. His hands demanded, traveling curves and slopes until somehow he found himself on his feet walking her toward the desk. The hands clutching at his shoulders spurred him forward until he pinned her against the edge. At that point, her hips molded to his, and there was no turning back.

Afterward, behind the closed doors of his office, he sat in his chair cradling a disheveled Delilah in a mirror image of Saturday night. Only where on Saturday night his soul had felt peace, all he felt now was guilt. Guilt and more self-loathing than he thought possible.

She offered and he took and took and took, knowing he could never give her the commitment she wanted.

Groaning, he jammed his fingers in his hair, tugging hard to ground himself. The action shifted his position, disturbing Delilah from her daze. She made a purring noise against the crook of his neck, the sound reverberating all the way to his core.

"Graphics must be wondering where the final copy is," he said. His voice was as dull and dead as he felt inside.

Delilah whimpered and nuzzled closer. "Who's the clear head this time?"

Certainly not him, or they wouldn't be here. "Mayor's waiting."

"S'pose you're right." Giving a little stretch, she sat up. The sight of her with her shirt half-unbuttoned was almost enough for him to weaken again. Almost.

"Work first, pleasure later. And then later again." She leaned in to kiss him, only to pull back when his spine stiffened. "What's wrong?"

It was time to man up and pay for what he'd done. "This is wrong," he told her.

After his symphony of mixed signals, he couldn't blame her for looking confused.

"What's wrong? Making love in the office? Neither of us planned—"

"Having sex period," he replied. Purposely using the coarser word to make his point.

"I see." Her face crumbled with understanding. "Well then, I better get those copy edits down to graphics."

Climbing off his lap, she straightened her clothing. Despicable as he felt, Simon couldn't help his burst of admiration at the way she pushed her hurt and confusion aside with a tuck of her hair. Then he thought of her history, and regretted having to make her play strong yet again.

He was about to apologize when the phone on his desk jangled, breaking the unsettled atmosphere. "That's probably the art department now. You should answer. We wouldn't want to keep them waiting."

Simon grabbed her wrist. "Don't go yet," he said. "Not this way."

He held fast while barking orders to the employee on the other end of the line. He'd apologize for being abrupt tomorrow. The only thing that mattered at the moment was Delilah. Touching her might have been a mistake; his arm itched to tug her close. But what end would that serve? She deserved intimacy and like he said, all he could ever give her was sex.

As soon as he hung up, she tried to pull free. "You can let go now. I stayed."

He didn't want to release her—it could be the last time he touched her—but he had no choice. "I didn't want you walking out thinking you did something wrong," he told her.

"Nice of you, seeing as how I didn't think I had."

He winced, the sharpness deserved. "What I meant was, I didn't want you thinking I regretted what just happened."

Again, his words were failing him. Her eyes narrowed. "Funny but the phrase 'this was wrong' sure seems regretful."

"Please, Delilah, you have to know my regrets have nothing to do with what we've done together. This weekend or today."

"Go on." She folded her arms across her chest. Still glaring, but she was listening.

Now the hard part. To explain. He turned to the window. If he couldn't see her eyes, speaking would be easier. "I thought I'd be fine going back to Boston," he said, looking out. "For crying out loud, the…hazing… was fifteen years ago. I'd filed it away. Only when we landed did it come flooding back.

Every time I turned around someone was saying something or there was a reminder."

"Like Jim's comment at the University Club."

"That started everything unraveling. It was all I could do to keep the memories at bay. Then I looked in your eyes on the dock and for a moment I felt calm. You were a human lifeline and I grabbed."

He knew she was thinking of how close they came to kissing that night. "Glad I could be of service," she drawled.

Against his better judgment, he looked over his shoulder. Delilah stood where he had left her, her arms tight across her chest. Her face was a stony mask. It killed him to see how easily he'd erased the loving, gentle woman he'd held moments earlier.

"That's the point. I knew immediately what I was doing was wrong. I had no business being attracted to you. Not—" he held up a hand "—because of who you are, but because of who I am. You were a walking, talking reminder of what I don't deserve."

She sighed. "You're talking about the hazing again."

"I'm talking about *you*. The kind of woman you are."

"What kind is that?"

He had to turn back to the window. Outside, the sky had grown gray; the sun gone from view. "Spectacular," he said in a reverent voice. "Hit me like a ton of bricks Sunday morning." He could still remember the way his stomach clenched when he woke to find her smiling next to the bed.

"Wait a minute. Sunday morning? You sent me home Sunday morning. I spent an entire day trying to figure out why you shut down."

"That was a mistake," he admitted. "At the time I wasn't sure what else to do."

"Here's a clue. You could have talked to me." Suddenly she was in his view, her eyes hot with anger. "You could have told me what you were thinking."

"I didn't know what to say. I figured it would be better to buy some time until I could sort out the words."

"Is that so? Twenty-four hours of putting me through hell and the best you came up with was 'this is wrong' *after* we made love?"

Why did she keep using that word? "We didn't make—"

"Yes, we did!" she spat. "*I* did."

"Which is exactly why I had to back away!" Her declaration struck like a fist. Couldn't she see he backed away to avoid those words, to save her from saying them? "For God's sake, Delilah, you believe in soul mates and missing puzzle pieces. You want a relationship that promises happily ever after. I can't give you those things. I can't be anyone's soul mate."

He watched as his words struck her and prayed she would someday understand he was doing this for her. "The part of me worthy of that right doesn't exist anymore," he said. "There's too much damage."

"Oh, for crying out loud, Simon, when are you going to realize the past doesn't matter to me?"

"I *am* my past!" he roared. "Don't you get it?" Hands balling to fists, he broke away before he struck the wall. "When those guys... When I let those guys... I killed the real Simon Cartwright. He stopped existing and all that was left was this person pretending to be human. You slept with a shell, Delilah. A really charming, pathetic coward."

"Damn you," Delilah replied. How dare he stand there hurling the same words he hurled at the beach when not a single one of them was true. "You were not a coward that day. You were a scared child."

He shook his head. Without looking at his

face, she knew he'd shut his eyes and his ears to what she was trying to say. It only made her angrier. "You had no right to shut me out of this relationship."

"I just want you to have what you deserve."

"What I—" She shook her head. "Who are you to decide what I do and do not deserve? That is my call to make. Do you understand that? *I* decide who I want to be with and I decide which Simon Cartwright is the one I love. Do you understand me? Not you, not those bastards who raped you in the ninth grade. Me."

Simon sucked in his breath.

The word just flew out. As soon as she heard the noise, she knew she'd crossed the line. Angry as she was, Delilah could kick herself. Simon could barely say the word *hazing,* he was nowhere near hearing the ugly truth. She'd just been so damn mad. Why couldn't the stubborn fool see that he was so much more than what happened that day?

Whatever opportunity she might have had to convince him was over. When he turned, his face was as cold a mask as she'd ever seen. He thrust a stack of papers at her. "You better get these down to graphics," he told her. "They're waiting for them."

She slammed the office door on her way out.

CHAPTER TEN

DELILAH'S PHONE RANG every five minutes the entire way home. She ignored the calls. She wasn't in the mood to update Chloe or Larissa and she knew it wasn't Simon calling. Even if by some miracle it was him, she thought as she jammed the key into her building's front door, he could go to blazes. *This was wrong.*

She hated him. Hated him so badly her heart felt like someone stomped on it.

Oh wait, someone did.

For the second time in four days, she was going to bed haunted by Simon's touch. Only this time there wouldn't be a repeat occurrence. Not unless he suddenly realized he wasn't protecting her heart by walking away.

Her phone started ringing again. "For crying out loud, this is ridiculous." She fished the foolish thing out of her bag. "What?"

"Delilah?"

Great. Just what she needed. "Hey, Mom."

"Is something wrong? You sounded upset when you answered."

Delilah could feel a smile kicking into her voice automatically. Ready for another round of "everything is wonderful." "I…"

Not this time. She was tired of pretending everything was wonderful just so her mother wouldn't be sad. Why should she get a free pass when Delilah didn't? "Actually, Mom, things are pretty lousy right now."

"What happened? Did something go wrong on your business trip?"

"Oh no! My business trip was fantastic," she drawled. "Best seventy-two hours of my life." She punctuated the sentence by slapping her pocketbook on the coffee table. "It's all your fault, too. You and your stupid missing pieces and soul mates. They're a joke. They sound so wonderful and romantic, but they're just big fat lies."

Plopping down on her sofa, she kicked at the throw pillows to make room for her legs. Was she being fair? Probably not, but she didn't care. Simon's rejection crushed her and she wanted someone else to feel as bad as she did. After all these years of wearing a happy face for her benefit, her mother had earned the honor.

On the other end of the line, she heard her mother let out a long breath. "Do you feel better now?"

"You'd like me to say so, wouldn't you?"

"Only if it's true."

Delilah barely contained her snort. "Right."

"Is that what you think about me? That I don't want to listen to your problems?"

"'All I want is to know everyone is happy,'" she quoted. "Isn't that what you always say?"

"Because I'm your mother. It would break my heart to see one of you suffering."

"And we all know what would happen then."

On the other end of the line, her mother gasped. "Oh, Delilah…" she started in a sad, shaky voice. "When your father died, I…"

"I know." She didn't need to hear the story again. Her anger was already giving way to a heap-load of guilt. One sharp conversation and her mother broke.

"I was going to say, when he died, I handled losing him pretty badly. It wasn't fair of me. You kids were your father's greatest achievement and I let you all down. I let him down. I just missed him so much."

Delilah was stunned. The last thing she expected was for her mother to agree. She plucked at the piping on the cushion, feeling a new heaviness. "We missed him, too."

"I know. And I'm sorry that instead of getting to grieve your father, you had to help handle my grief. I should never have let that happen. Now it looks like I have something else to be sorry for, too. I never meant for you to feel like you had to pretend to be happy."

She never told them not to. "Didn't you think it was odd I never had any problems?" Delilah asked her.

"Honestly? I was simply proud of how together you seemed to be." When Delilah didn't comment, she must have felt the silent prodding, because she added, "All right, maybe I liked the fact you only had good news. It made life easier."

"Same on this end. I always thought keeping a false front was easy, but I don't know now." Delilah let her head fall back. "All this honesty is exhausting."

Although her mother certainly didn't collapse into tears the way Delilah expected. Maybe it was okay to admit life wasn't perfect.

She wondered if she could get Simon to realize the same truth.

Thinking about Simon ruined her mood more and she sighed.

"So," her mother said, clearly hearing, "what's this about soul mates?"

"I'm sorry about that. I shouldn't have gone off on you." It wasn't her mother's fault the man she thought was her missing piece didn't believe he fit.

"Do you really think the whole concept is a lie?"

"No," Delilah conceded. She believed the concept with all her heart. That was the problem. "But what do you do when your soul mate is afraid to be with you."

"I would say he's not really your soul mate then."

Hard to imagine. She loved Simon more than she thought possible. Even tonight, angry as she was with him, she loved him.

"I can't picture my life with anyone else," she told her. "Worst part is I know he cares about me, too. He says he's pushing me away because it's 'for the best.'"

"Maybe it is. Just because we love someone doesn't mean the relationship is meant to be."

Delilah's heart sank at the thought. "No offense, Mom," she grumbled, "but you're lousy at heart-to-hearts."

"Why? Because I'm not telling you what you want to hear?"

Ouch. Burned by her own mother. "He thinks I don't know the real him, but I do. When I think of what Simon went through—"

"Wait a second, *Simon?* As in Simon Cartwright? What kind of business trip was this?"

"A real business trip," she shot back. "Doesn't matter anyway. Simon doesn't think he's worthy of a committed relationship and nothing I can say will change his mind."

"I'm sorry, sweetheart."

"Tell me about it." She sank lower into her cushions. For a second, she was ten years old again, needing a hug to make everything better. "I'm sorry about yelling."

"Don't be. I obviously needed to hear it. Besides, you're not doing anyone any good by keeping everything inside."

Simon's closed-off expression flashed before her eyes. "I'm not sure speaking up did me any favors, either. I said some things I shouldn't have said when Simon and I were arguing and might have made things worse." There certainly couldn't have been more space between them in his office tonight if she'd tried.

On the other end, she could tell by her

mother's deep breath she wanted to say something. "What?"

"Did I ever tell you about Amanda Beary?"

"No." Not that she cared at this moment either.

"She was a girl in your father's econ class. Absolutely gorgeous in that milkmaid, farm-fresh kind of way. Half the school had the hots for her—your father included. About a month after your dad and I started dating, she asked him out."

"And he turned her down."

"No, he came to me, and told me he was 'conflicted.' I think that's the word he used. I told him that he had to either be one hundred percent with me or not at all. In the end he decided his fantasy girl wasn't worth losing what we had."

More proof they'd been meant to be together. Just what she didn't need. "It's a sweet story, Mom, but what's going on with Simon isn't so simple."

"Maybe not, but the point's the same. Either a person is your soul mate or he isn't. If the two of you are meant to be, you'll find your way back to each other."

Delilah was willing to bet the person who coined the phrase "meant to be" never threw her lover's sexual assault in his face when they were arguing.

It'd be nice to say the long-overdue conversation made her feel better, but after hanging up with her mother, all Delilah wanted to do was cry. Largely because her mother had been right. Either she and Simon were meant to be together or they weren't. So long as Simon failed to see his attack made him more of a man, not less, Delilah had to lean toward *weren't*.

Since leaving the office, tears had threatened to spill over onto her cheeks. She let one slip through. The way she saw the situation, she had two options. She could maintain the status quo. Go to work every day, act like her heart wasn't breaking and hope Simon had an epiphany.

She might as well have the word *welcome* tattooed on her forehead while she was at it. As much as she loved Simon, she couldn't go back to being his faithful assistant while he collected society dates. Not after being his lover.

Meaning she had no choice but to select option two.

* * *

"Are you sure?" Larissa asked her the next morning.

"No." She couldn't be less sure of anything, but neither could she see any other way.

"Maybe if you gave him a few more days. He might change his mind."

She smiled at her friend's wishful thinking. "I'd need a lot more than a few days for that." Lying alone in her bed last night, she'd realized the only thing that could change Simon was Simon himself. Who knew if that would ever happen.

In the meantime, she couldn't afford to stick around to find out.

"If I stay, there's too much chance I'll repeat the same mistakes," she told Larissa.

"I understand, but do you have to quit the agency altogether? Couldn't you simply transfer to a different department? CMT's a big company."

Run by Simon. "You and I both know we'd be running into each other all the time." Nothing but torment as far as Delilah was concerned. If she was going to move forward, she needed a clean break. "I'm better off quitting the agency altogether."

"This place won't be the same without you,"

her blond-haired friend said. "Who's going to help me deal with Chloe's crazy crushes?"

"You'll be fine. It's not as though I'm moving back to Kansas. I'll be a text message away. Plus, look on the bright side, now that I'm unemployed, I'm have more time for bridesmaid's duty."

Larissa laughed and held out her arms. "Well, when you put it that way..."

She pulled Delilah into her embrace. "Remember we're here for you no matter what," she whispered in Delilah's ear.

Delilah found herself fighting back tears. Despite paying it cool and confident for Larissa, on the inside she was scared to death. Not only was she walking away from the man she loved, she was jumping back into the job pool, too. There was a good shot she'd end up with nothing.

She tightened her grip on Larissa. "Thanks," she whispered back.

Then, taking a deep breath, she walked down the corridor to Simon's office.

One last time.

She found Simon's door ajar and him arranging the objects on his desk into straight lines. Naturally fate had to give one last stab by having him look more handsome than ever. His fawn-colored suit and pastel shirt were impossibly light. She wondered if he chose the combination on purpose to signal a new start. He'd gone swimming this morning, as well. His collar bore the telltale dampness.

Once upon a time, she would have knocked for fear of approaching him unaware, but not today. "We need to talk," she said.

A minute ticked by before he lifted his eyes. His expression remained closed to her, same as last night. "This isn't the time," he said.

"I only need a minute. You owe me as much after last night," she added, shutting the door.

He looked about to argue only to reconsider. "Fine," he said, attention focused on straightening his stapler. "Say your piece. It won't change my mind."

"If I thought it would, I'd remind you that multiple people against one isn't a fair fight, and that I couldn't picture anyone—let alone a fifteen-year-old boy—fighting under those circumstances."

Even from across the room, Delilah could see his jaw muscles clench. "If you're finished…" He turned away from her and began busying himself with his laptop.

"I quit," she said.

There, job done. What followed was silence while Simon sat staring at his laptop.

"If you're sure," he finally said.

He didn't even try to muster a protest. Delilah's last spark of hope flickered and died. Maybe her mother was right; maybe she and Simon weren't meant to be. Maybe he was nothing more than a blip on her way to lifelong happiness. Heavy as her heart felt at the moment, she didn't think so.

One thing she did know was that if she had to walk away—and Simon's inaction said she did—then she wasn't walking away without the last word. Not this time.

"I love you, Simon," she told him.

He immediately stood up and walked to the window. Putting his back to her, as though that would block the words. "Don't."

"Too late. My feelings aren't going to change. You can tell me how unworthy you are, you can turn your back, you can swim a million laps to forget, but none of those things will change how I feel. How I'll always feel. Believe me, I wish I could be like you, but I can't forget this weekend happened—that *we* happened. I'll tell you something else, too…"

While she'd been speaking, she'd crossed the room, forcing herself into his line of vision. She wanted him to see her when she said the next part. "What happened fifteen years ago doesn't matter to me. If anything, what you endured made me love you more."

"You can't," he said. His voice was soft, barely audible. That and the bright sheen in his eyes were the only signs her words meant anything. The rest of his face was an expressionless mask.

"But I do. You say you're this broken shell, a coward hiding behind charm. Maybe that's true, but it doesn't matter to me. I still love you. Broken pieces and all. And I hate that you think you're not worth my love because you are worth every damn ounce of feeling I have and more. Someday I hope you realize that."

More silence. With every word not spoken, her goodbye gained resolve. "If, or until that happens, I can't be around you. As much as I love you, I can't be your doormat."

"I would never..." But his sentence drifted off. He knew as well as she did the argument wouldn't hold. So long as he tried to pretend their love affair didn't happen, he would be stepping on her heart. Not on purpose, but stepping all the same. "I'm sorry."

"I'm sorry, too. For a lot of things." Sorry

she had to leave, sorry he was letting her walk away. Sorry he couldn't see the truth about himself.

There wasn't much more for her to say. She longed to brush her fingers across his cheek one more time, but held herself in check. Touching would only make the separation more painful. God knew her heart hurt enough already.

"Goodbye, Simon. If you ever decide to forgive yourself let me know."

She started to walk away only to have one last thought she needed to share before she left. "You call yourself a coward for not fighting that day. Refusing to fight when you're outnumbered isn't cowardice, Simon, it's self-preservation. But letting those bastards keep you from having a true and full life now... If you ask me, that's more cowardly than anything that happened in prep school."

With that, she closed the door between them.

Simon couldn't remember when the click of a door had sounded so loud. He stared at the smooth oak grain, silence roaring in his ears, and counted. One. Two. Three...

The door remained closed. Delilah didn't come back.

A hand squeezed his chest, sucking the air from his lungs. He wanted to chase her down and beg her to stay. But his feet stayed rooted. It was for the best, her leaving. If she stayed, he'd have only hurt her again. Now at least she could find someone else. A man who could love her the way the way she deserved to be loved.

It's for the best, he repeated. *For the best.* The hand squeezed tighter. Black seeped into his line of vision, obliterating everything but the closed door.

It was for the best.

Son-of-a—! He grabbed the first item he could and hurled it against the door. The stapler. It smashed and broke in two, leaving behind an ugly gash in the wood.

CHAPTER ELEVEN

OH, FOR CRYING out loud. For the third time that day Simon shoved his chair away from his desk because the file he needed wasn't in the system.

"Anna!" If his voice sounded suspiciously like a bellow, he didn't care. "Why isn't the first quarter buy in the system yet?"

He heard the squeak of chair wheels as he rounded the corner and found his new assistant already facing the doorway. Her eyes were wide with nerves. Big brown eyes that did not evoke sympathy. "I—I don't know," she stuttered. "I uploaded the new version this morning, just like you asked me to."

Simon sighed. "Did you remember to double click Save this time?" The way her face fell was the only answer he needed.

"Sorry, I'll upload the file now."

"Please," he told her. "I'll be waiting." For

quite a while, too, if the way she was searching through the clump of papers on her desk was any indication.

"By the way," she called, stopping him from leaving. "Virginia called." Virginia being Bartlett's vice president of marketing. "She wanted to set up a meeting to discuss the company's NBA campaign."

"Did you?"

Anna's eyes widened again. "Um, you were on the phone at the time. I wanted to find out who else should be included."

Since sighing a second time would only make the girl more jittery, Simon settled for gripping the top of her cubicle wall. Delilah would have handled the entire thing on her own.

He reminded himself that Anna was new and still adjusting to his idiosyncrasies.

She also wasn't Delilah.

"Schedule the meeting based on her schedule. We'll coordinate who should attend later," he told her. "And upload that media buy."

"Which do you want me to do first?"

Heaven help him. "Both."

He headed back to his office, wondering how late this setback would keep him at the office. Not that he minded the extra work these days. Just as the board had hoped, the Bartlett account was a major boon for CMT. In addition to avoiding layoffs, all three offices had to hire additional staffing to accommodate the increased workload. The board was so thrilled that his father had actually used the word *proud*.

Funny how his father's pride always seemed to be inversely proportionate to how fraudulent Simon felt. Oh, sure, from the outside, the agency looked to be more successful than ever. They couldn't see how unsteady Simon felt. Day in, day out he struggled to find solid footing. It was as though he was trying to walk on top of the swimming pool. His new assistant's inability to read his mind only compounded the unsettled feeling.

Delilah could read his mind. From the very start she had this uncanny ability to know what he needed. Even in resigning. He'd been shocked to find out she'd called Jim Bartlett to let him know she'd taken a new position, going so far as to word her lie the exact way he'd planned to. Then again, he really wasn't surprised at all.

"I have to admit," Bartlett had said when he told Simon about the call, "I was looking forward to her being part of the team. You two had a real rapport. But I'm sure whoever replaces her will be equally good."

No one would replace her, Simon had wanted to say. She was the best assistant he'd ever had.

Delilah was the best period.

God, he missed her like breathing. Every day for the past two weeks, she'd been everywhere he looked. Walking past the filing cabinets, he'd see her ponytailed head bent over a drawer. Her laugh would drift to him from the back of the elevator. Hell, while swimming the other day he swore he saw her shiny black flats waiting for him by the pool's edge. He kept telling himself letting her go had been for the best. Every time, he heard her parting words mocking his choice. *To let those bastards keep you from having a full and true life. That's the real cowardice.*

Coming around the corner, he nearly drew to a stop. *Crap.* As if his day couldn't be worse, Chloe Abrams stood chatting with one of the other account assistants. She didn't speak to him directly, but he could feel her eyes on him.

He pretended they weren't trying to freeze holes in his body and smiled. "Good afternoon, Chloe. We haven't seen much of you lately."

What was he thinking? They hadn't seen much of her because she wasn't here visiting Delilah. A fact Chloe jumped on immediately. "Not much reason to be on this floor anymore, is there?" Simon wondered if his smile looked as false as hers. "I was just leaving."

"Actually…" *Don't do it,* the voice in his head screamed. *Don't open the wound more than it's open already.* But he had to. He needed to know how Delilah was doing. If she'd moved on.

"Before you go, could I have a word with you in my office?"

"Something you need, Mr. Cartwright?" she asked as soon as soon as he closed them inside.

Simon hesitated. From the glint in Chloe's eyes, she knew exactly what he wanted. In a way, he was glad. It saved him having to try and be subtle. "Have you talked to Delilah lately?"

"We had drinks last night as a matter of fact."

"She's doing okay?"

The brunette quirked a smile. "About as

well as can be expected, considering the circumstances."

Considering, Simon silently repeated. Still, he needed more. Problem was, the questions he wanted to ask—Was she missing him? Did she still love him?—weren't questions he had a right to ask. "Is she working?"

"Not yet. She's had a couple interviews, but nothing's come of them yet."

"Something will break for her soon. She's too good..." Breaking off, he walked toward his desk. "Would you tell her that if she needs a reference or if I can make any calls on her behalf..."

"No offense, but I don't think she wants anything from you."

Couldn't blame her there. "She's still angry, then." Such an obvious thing to say.

"Angry?" Chloe replied. Out of the corner of his eye, Simon caught the end of her shrug. "More like sad. Really, deeply sad."

So was Simon. He reminded himself yet again Delilah's leaving was for the best. The more time passed, the less weight those words carried.

Behind him, Chloe could be heard nervously shifting her weight. "Is there anything else?" she asked him. "Otherwise, I should get back downstairs."

"Of course," he replied. "Thank you.

"Chloe!" He spoke up just as she was about to walk out. "Would you tell her..." Tell her what? Anything he wanted to say would only make the situation more painful for both of them. "Never mind."

She gave him a long, scrutinizing look that made his skin itch and for a second he thought she might say something back. He was wrong. She gave a quick nod, and slipped out the door.

Give it a few more days, he said when his chest started to hurt. *Things will improve.*

A few days became another week and the pain lingered. At the month mark, Anna and her frightened eyes were replaced by Leon who, while far more organized, still didn't fit quite right.

The mark left by the stapler reminded him that no one would. Because no matter how skilled or efficient his next assistant may be, he or she would never fit as perfectly as Delilah.

He still saw her ghost in the office and at night, when he collapsed in his empty bed, it was her voice he heard whispering in his head.

That night, after another tedious charity event with another insipid date, Simon took a long look at himself in the mirror. In his reflection, he saw what the rest of the world saw: a successful, powerful businessman. A mover and a shaker, one of the industry magazines called him. He'd always considered those compliments false, knowing as he did that beneath the accomplished exterior lay the truth—that he was nothing more than a scared, scarred nerd of a kid pretending to be a better man than he was.

You only see what happened to you; I see how you rose above it. He rubbed the back of his neck while snatches of Delilah's words repeated themselves over and over. *Not to have a full and true life. You rose above.*

Had he? Risen above? Delilah certainly believed so. Said she loved him even. Flaws and all.

Exhausted, he let his head fall against the mirror. *You, Simon Cartwright, are an idiot.* Delilah *loved* him. A lifetime of happiness was his for the asking if he had the guts to take it.

Delilah was right. He was being a coward. And it was high time he stop.

Suddenly he knew where he had to go. It was time he visited the past once and for all.

The building hadn't changed much in fifteen years. The gray shingles were still pale and mossy, the walls still worn and weather-beaten. In fact, the only significant change was the padlock dangling from the latch.

Fortune was on his side. The lock was open. Inside, the place had changed even less. Sculls lined the sides, life jackets hung on the walls. Someone had painted the letters BNA in bright blue on the peak over the riverfront door, in case rowers forgot which school they represented.

Simon got halfway to the door when the shaking started. Beginning from deep inside, and rippling outward like waves on the shore, they kicked the knees out from under him, knocking him to the ground. As he clung to his middle, he realized why. It was here, on this very spot. Details came rushing back, memories he'd tried so hard to drown. He saw their eyes, heard Chip's drunken laugh. *Where you going, freshman? The party's just started...* And he saw his teenage self, standing in the same spot, arms pinned behind his back so he couldn't escape. He remembered now. He'd tried to struggle. He'd begged. They wouldn't let him go.

"No," he groaned at the memories. "No, no!" His fist pounded the wooden floor in time with the chant. "No!" he screamed. Over and over until all the rage and humiliation he'd pushed down deep boiled over in a long, anguished scream.

When the final rageful sound had pushed it way out, he collapsed to the ground. Lungs raw, tears staining his cheeks, he grabbed his knees and he let himself cry. He cried for the boy whose childhood died that day and he cried for the boy who wasn't allowed to grow up whole. For the man he became. The shattered, guarded man whose heart wanted so badly to let someone in. And he cried for all the years he lost to fearing this memory. He cried until there were no more tears left to cry, and all he could do was lie there and listen to the sound of his ragged breathing filling the musty air.

Little by little, his breathing eased, revealing another sound. *Splat-splish. Splat-splish.* Below the floor the river lapped the shoreline.

Fifteen years ago he'd heard the same

rhythm. It had entered his soul, soothed his anguish. In that sound he'd found the strength to get up and go on with his life. For fifteen years he let what happened in this building define him and in doing so, he'd failed to see the rest of the definition. Delilah was right; the boy he called a coward had a lot more strength than he gave him credit for.

Drying his eyes, he lay and listened. Lap by lap, the river began to wash away the dirt and shame, filling the cracks of his shattered soul. Simon closed his eyes, and tried to imagine the pieces coming together. What he saw was a pair of soft, welcoming eyes the color water should be. One by one, the pieces snapped back in place, until all that was left was one Delilah-shaped hole.

I love you. Broken pieces and all.

What a fool he'd been. So much time wasted.

He hoped it wasn't too late.

With his hands shaking, he fished his phone out of his pocket and dialed the office. "Leon," he barked, "I need you to put me through to either Chloe Abrams or Larissa Boyd. I don't care which one. Whichever one you can reach first. And tell whoever answers it's urgent."

* * *

"I've narrowed my decision to two choices. Which one do you like? Historical Long Island or Mexican destination?"

Chloe picked up the first of two brochures Larissa had laid on the restaurant table. "Shouldn't Tom be helping you make the decision?"

"He's no help. Every time I ask him, he says, 'It's up to you.' Which one do you like best, Delilah? Del?" She waved a hand in front of Delilah's face. "Are you there?"

"Sorry," Del replied. "What was the question?"

"Which venue do you like?"

"Shouldn't Tom be helping you pick one?"

On the other side of the table, her friends exchanged a look. Realizing the question had already been asked, Delilah apologized again. "I guess my mind wandered," she told them.

"No kidding," Larissa told her. "You've been spacing out all night."

"I'm sorry about that too." She picked at the corner of her Bartlett's Ale label. Why she ordered the brand in the first place, other than for strictly masochistic reasons, was beyond her. She didn't even like the stuff all that much.

"I guess weddings aren't my favorite topic at the moment. Or anything else remotely related to romance for that matter. Yesterday I got teary-eyed at a fabric softener commercial."

"Exactly why we dragged you out tonight," Chloe said. "It's been a month since you quit. You can't keep staying holed up in your apartment. It's not healthy."

"I go out."

"For job interviews. How'd today's go by the way?"

"Good." The label tore. She stripped off a long, thin line. "Placement agency thinks they'll offer me the job."

"Fantastic!" Larissa exclaimed.

She supposed. The job was with a smaller, midtown agency. Nothing at all like CMT. Actually, none of the agencies Delilah had interviewed with had been like CMT.

Because none of the other agencies had Simon.

Delilah suppressed a sigh. She always considered herself a resilient person, but hard as she might try, she couldn't move on. Four weeks later and she still spent her days fighting memories. Since walking out of his office, she'd seen Simon's face twice. Both times it was in the gossip columns. In both pictures, the women he escorted wore huge, happy smiles. But really, who wouldn't smile having Simon hold them? Lord knows, she'd beamed all that Saturday night.

In the pictures though, Simon's smile didn't reach his eyes.

That sad expression…that was the reason she couldn't let go. It killed her not to know how he was doing. Chloe and Larissa wouldn't tell her. She'd made them promise not to, and they were, unfortunately, honoring her request. Lack of information was killing her. For all she knew the sadness in Simon's photos was a product of her imagination.

One thing was certain. She definitely had a new appreciation for her mother's grief. Delilah's insides felt like someone had cut a three-mile-wide hole through the center. Too big to be filled by anyone not named Simon Cartwright.

She had the bad feeling she was about to follow in her mother's footsteps. Spending the rest of her life half-living and alone.

Shoving her beer bottle aside, she reached for her pocketbook. "I'm sorry," she said for the third time. "I appreciate what you're doing, but I'm not going to be very good company. How about we take a rain—"

"No!" Larissa interrupted. "You can't go. Right, Chloe?"

"Right," Chloe agreed. "We need to celebrate your potential job."

"I promise we'll celebrate if I get the offer." Right now she wanted nothing more than to curl up and go to sleep.

"But I need some advice about barista boy."

Delilah might have believed her if she didn't see Larissa nudge Chloe with her shoulder. Having seen it, however, the hair on the back of her neck began prickling. "All right, you two, what's going on?" she asked. "Why are you so desperate to keep me here at the bar?"

"I asked them to."

Delilah swore her heart stopped. Sure enough. There, at the table's edge, stood Simon. Rumpled and unshaven, he looked like he hadn't slept in days.

Her first instinct was to leap to her feet. She didn't. Instead she turned her eyes on the two sheepish women sitting with her.

"Don't be mad," Larissa said. "We didn't tell you because we were afraid you wouldn't come."

"I'm not mad," Delilah replied. She didn't

know what to feel. Scared. Hopeful. A zillion emotions rolled around inside her.

"Good," Chloe said. "Because we'd head-slap you if you were." As she slipped out of the booth, she gave Delilah's shoulder a squeeze. "Hear him out," she whispered. "He misses you."

And she missed him. Simply reappearing in her life, however, wasn't enough. She was done chasing while he ran away.

"So you got my friends to help trick me," she said once Chloe and Larissa vanished. "Whatever you told them must have been pretty convincing. Chloe's a hard sell."

"I told her the truth. I wanted to talk with you. I miss you."

Missed her, huh? "Funny, I didn't hear my phone ringing."

"I didn't think you'd take my calls."

"Of course I'd have taken them," she said, reaching for her beer. He knew darn well she'd take them. She only declared her love on the way out the door.

A hand plucked the bottle from her fingers. "It's Five O'Clock Somewhere?"

"What can I say? I've acquired a taste." He returned the bottle, but no longer thirsty, she set it out of reach. "You said you wanted to talk with me? What about?"

"Do you mind if I sit?"

"Go ahead."

She gestured for him to take a seat on the other side of the booth, but to her surprise he slid next to her, drawing so close they touched thigh to thigh. "I went back," he told her.

Back? Until this moment, she'd refused to give him a second look, but hearing his statement, her head shot up. "You mean?"

"To the boathouse." He picked up her bottle and took a long drink. "After you quit, I couldn't stop thinking about what you said. About me being a coward."

"I should never have said—"

"Don't apologize. You were right." He shifted so he could face her. Delilah was shocked to find his eyes clear and bright without a trace of the anguish she expected. "I was being a coward. Not then. Now. I spent all these years beating myself up for something that wasn't my fault. I don't want to beat myself up anymore."

"I'm so glad," she whispered. Maybe now, finally, he could let himself heal.

A tear had slipped down her cheek. She moved to brush it aside, only to feel the warmth of Simon's touch. "Me too," he told her. "I'm done running away from what I want."

It was Delilah's turn to be afraid. She'd misread his words before, only to have her hopes dashed. She needed to hear him say the words. And so she held her breath.

Simon's thumb fanned her cheek. "I want you, Delilah."

"You—you do?" A lump rose in her throat making it hard to speak. How badly she wanted to believe him, but the words still sounded too good to be real.

"Swear to God." Still cupping her cheek, Simon took her hand and pressed it to his chest. "I want to be the man I was this weekend. Not the advertising superstar, not the winning son, but the guy who went shopping and ate pizza and let a woman get close to him for the first time in his life. I want to be a real man, Delilah, and I can't do that without you."

Delilah couldn't believe her ears. "What about everything you said about being too damaged for a relationship?"

"I am damaged. I've got a ton of demons and anyone with half a brain would tell you that's a red flag for any relationship. But…"

He kissed her. A long slow kiss. "I love you, Delilah," he whispered. "From the moment you walked out of my office, there's been this giant hole in my chest where my heart should be. You're the only woman who can fill it. Ever. As damaged as I am, I'd be far more damaged without you. You make me whole, Delilah St. Germain.

"So please," he continued, searching her face with anxious uncertainty, "please tell me it's not too late."

His image blurred, and she had to squeeze her eyes tight before tears spilled free. The courage it took for Simon to speak from his heart…it humbled her to think he took that risk for her. This man, this sexy, charismatic, brave, broken man, loved her. What a wonderful gift.

"Never," she whispered. "It could never be too late. Because you make me whole, too."

"Thank God." He crushed her to him, his kiss the perfect punctuation point of every emotion he'd shared. Her arms wrapping around him, Delilah kissed him with all the love she held in her heart, letting him know his risk had been rewarded.

"I love you," she told him when they broke

apart. "There is no other man in this world I could ever want."

"You sure? I've still got demons to fight."

"Who doesn't?" Frankly, she didn't care how damaged he thought he might be. Nothing was so broken that it couldn't be fixed. That they were in each other's arms was proof of that.

"Then, there's one more thing I need to do." Her whimper as he pulled out of her embrace quickly turned into a gasp when he knelt on the barroom floor. "This isn't the most romantic place in the world, and I don't have a ring, but if you'll have me, I will spend the rest of our lives together making sure you know how special you are to me."

"I don't need to be special," Delilah said, sniffing back the tears. "I just need you."

Simon smiled. "That, sweetheart, you already have."

As he pulled her into his embrace, Delilah's heart grew fuller than she could ever imagine. The completeness of finding the person you knew would be by your side for the rest of her life.

Off in the distance, she swore she heard a *click*.

"Did you hear that?" she asked, pulling back?

"Hear what, sweetheart?"

"Nothing." Seeing the love shining in Simon's eyes, Delilah already knew the answer.

The final piece of the puzzle had just slipped into place.

"You made the paper again," Chloe announced. The tabloid landed on her desk with a *plop*. "Do you have to look so freaking happy?"

Delilah laughed. A photo of her and Simon sat just below the society page headline. "CMT Honcho Simon Cartwright and his fiancée, Delilah St. Germain…" she read. She didn't think she'd ever get tired of reading those words.

Same as she'd never tire of seeing that smile light up Simon's eyes.

"We'll try to look miserable at the next event just for you, okay?" she teased.

"Don't you dare," Larissa said, handing over her cup of coffee. "We love seeing you so happy."

Deliriously happy, thought Delilah. Oh, sure, she and Simon still had their problems. Every couple did. But she wouldn't trade the problems—or the man she shared them with—for the world.

"La-Roo is right," Chloe said. "It's nice to know at least some people in this world have soul mates. Makes up for the rest of us."

"Just you wait, Chloe Abrams, your time is coming." After all, if she and Simon found their happy ever after, then anyone could. Like her mother always said, everyone's pot has a lid, every puzzle has its piece. She might not think so, but her cynical friend had a soul mate same as everyone else.

She saluted her friend with her cup. "Something tells me your other half is right around the corner."

* * * * *

LARGER-PRINT BOOKS!
GET 2 FREE LARGER-PRINT NOVELS PLUS
2 FREE GIFTS!

❦ HARLEQUIN®

Romance

From the Heart, For the Heart

*Here's a sneak peek at DARING TO TRUST THE BOSS
by Susan Meier*

SOMEHOW THEY'D ENDED up standing face-to-face again. Under the luxurious blanket of stars, next to the twinkling blue water, the only sound the slight hum of the filter for the pool.

He reached out and cupped the side of her face.

"You are a brave, funny woman, Miss Prentiss."

Though she knew it was dangerous to get too personal with him, especially since his nearness already had her heart thrumming and her knees weak, she was only human. And even if it was a teeny tiny inconsequential thing, she didn't want to give up the one innocent pleasure she was allowed to get from him.

She caught his gaze. "Olivia."

"Excuse me?"

"I like it when you call me Olivia."

He took a step closer. "Really?"

She shrugged, trying to make light of her request. "Everybody calls me Vivi. Sometimes it makes me feel six again. Being called Olivia makes me feel like an adult."

"Or a woman."

The way he said *woman* sent heat rushing through her. Once again, he'd seen right through her ploy and might even realize she was attracted to him—

Oh, who was she kidding? He *knew* she was attracted to him.

HREXP0114

But even as yearning nudged her to be bold, reality intruded. The guy she finally, finally wanted to trust was rich, sophisticated, so far out of her league she was lucky to be working for him. She knew better than to get romantically involved with someone like him.

She stepped back. "I wouldn't go that far."

He caught her hand and tugged her to him. "I would."

He kissed her so quickly that her knees nearly buckled and her brain reeled. She could have panicked. Could have told him to go slow because she hadn't done this in a while, or even stop because this was wrong. But nobody, no kiss, had ever made her feel the warm, wonderful, scary sensations saturating her entire being right now. Not just her body, but her soul.

His lips moved over hers smoothly, expertly, shooting fire and ice down her spine. Her breath froze in her chest. Then he opened his mouth over hers and her lips automatically parted.

The fire and ice shooting down her spine exploded in her middle, reminding her of where this would go if she didn't stop him. Now. She was so far out of Tucker's league, it was foolish to even consider kissing him.

She jerked away, stepped back. His glistening green eyes had narrowed with confusion. He didn't understand why she'd stopped him.

Longing warred with truth. If he could pretend their stations in life didn't matter, she could pretend. Couldn't she?

DARING TO TRUST THE BOSS
by Susan Meier
is available February 4, 2014,
wherever books and ebooks are sold!